For my fantasy loving family

DRAGON WARS

BLOOD BROTHERS

BOOK 1

CRAIG HALLORAN

DON'T FORGET YOUR FREE BOOKS!

Join my newsletter and receive three magnificent stories from my bestselling series for FREE!

Not to mention that you'll have direct access to my collection of over 80 books, including audiobooks and boxsets. FREE and .99 cents giveaways galore!

Sign up here!
WWW.DRAGONWARSBOOKS.COM

Finally, please leave a review of Blood Brothers-Book 1 when you finish. I've typed my fingers to the bone writing it and your reviews are a huge help!

BLOOD BROTHERS REVIEW LINK! THANKS!

Dragon Wars: Blood Brothers - Book 1

By Craig Halloran

Publisher's Note

This book is a work of fiction. Names, characters, places, and incidents either are the product of the author's imagination or are used fictitiously, and any resemblance to actual persons, living or dead, events, or locales is entirely coincidental.

 Created with Vellum

PROLOGUE

"Hunt down the striplings and return them to me," Black Frost ordered.

"Dead or alive?" Drysis replied.

"Any form or fashion will do."

She rose from one knee, bowed and said, "Your will is my will, Glorious One." She turned and strode toward the steps that led down from the rooftop of the ancient temple.

Black Frost's tremendous body overshadowed her. His commanding voice carried over the whistling winds when he said, "Drysis, do you know the penalty for failure?"

She stopped, looked back over her shoulder and without batting a lash she answered, "Death."

1 FARHOOK

JABBING PAIN IN GREY CLOAK'S SKULL WOKE HIM. Groaning, he opened his eyes. His heartbeat was pounding in his temples, and he reached up to rub the throbbing knot on the back of his head, but the heavy cuff and chains latched around his wrists prevented it. "Perfect. Just perfect," he muttered in a voice dripping with sarcasm.

He was sitting on the cold damp floor of a dungeon cell. His nostrils flared. "The smell of dungeon refuse. Is there anything more delightful? *Ack!*"

His gray eyes quickly adjusted to the dungeon setting's dim light, revealing that he was chained inside a cramped cell that was nothing more than a cave that had been dug out of the rock. The ceiling was very low, and a grid of steel bars trapped him inside. The cell seemed more like a large kennel rather than something made for men. He pinched his nose, looked at his chains, and shook his head.

Grey Cloak's chain was tethered to a steel ring stuck in the ground and ran through the steel ring from one of his wrist cuffs to the other. It was short, maybe two feet, giving him little room to move. He ran the chain through the ring in a sawing motion, and the tight cuffs bit into his wrists.

"I have to admit they did a fine job binding me up." He examined the metal cuff on his left wrist. The clasp was bolted on. "Hmmm... no thieves' tool can pick that. It's going to take something stronger."

With his bare foot, Grey Cloak kicked the person that was seated across from him. He was snoring quietly, his chin resting on his chest.

"Dyphestive, wake up!" Grey Cloak quietly demanded. He kicked him again. "Wake up!"

Rolling his neck from side to side, Dyphestive rubbed his eyes with his immense hands. When he lifted his head, he bumped it on the cave ceiling. "Ow." He tried to rub his head, but his chains wouldn't reach. Furrowing his eyebrows, he looked at Grey Cloak and said, "See what you did now?"

"Me?" Grey Cloak said. "If you weren't so slow, we would have gotten away."

"I'm not slow. I'm big. Just because someone is big, that doesn't make them slow," Dyphestive said. "Besides, you were the one that got caught in the net. I was trying to free you."

"No, I was waiting for you," Grey Cloak fired back. He locked his fingers on his chains, dug his heels into the floor, and tried to pull the ring. He grunted, and his arms shook, but he gasped when the ring shackling him to the floor didn't budge. He sighed. "We need to get out of here before they kill us. Try to rip your chains free."

"Don't change the subject. You erred, and you need to admit it," Dyphestive said. He tilted his head and looked at his large bare feet. "They took my boots. Why did they take my boots?"

"Maybe they were going to make a canoe out of them."

A raspy chuckle erupted from the small cell across from them. Grey Cloak and Dyphestive exchanged a glance and crawled as close to the bars as they could.

The cell on the other side was dark. The only source of light was from a torch that burned at the far end of that hall. Grey Cloak peered across the way and squinted. "Who is that over there? Show yourself. I have questions."

In a scratchy voice, the man said, "I don't think you are in any position to make demands, stripling."

Grey Cloak's keen elven sight soon let him make out a disheveled old man huddled in the corner of his cell. His hair was long and wild.

"Listen, hermit, you help us out, and we can help you

out. We can get you out of here." He shrugged at Dyphestive.

"What makes you think that I want to leave? Hmmm. I like it here. It's peaceful and quiet, at least until you came. I had this place all to myself. My own mansion with many, many rooms," the hermit said.

Grey Cloak rolled his eyes and said under his breath, "He's insane."

"Insane!" The hermit scurried out of his corner and pressed his bushy face to the bars. His piercing brown eyes had golden flecks inside them. He stuck his arm, which had scaly skin, through the bars, shook his fist at them, and said, "What do you striplings know about sanity? Hmm! What do you know about anything? What have you seen? Fifteen summers? Hmm... I know all. I am a king!"

"If you say so." Grey Cloak took a seat and leaned back against the wall. "It's good to know that we are among royalty, Your Majesty. Will the queen be stopping by today?"

"Fool!" the hermit screamed. "You are disrespectful! I've seen your kind. A fast talker. A slippery goose. Words laced with ridicule." The hermit spat. "Well, let me tell you. Let's see where your clever words get you. Will they get you out of your cell? Can they whisk you from your doom? Tell me, smart one!"

"Probably," Grey Cloak replied, leaning forward to put his pointed ears between his knees.

"Probably not, I say! They will kill you. Yes. Kill you. But it won't be a quick death. No, you will be the feast, the sacrifice to their idols. While you live, they will cut your fingers and toes off and feast on them." The hermit smacked his lips. "Crunch, crunch, crunch."

Grey Cloak's stomach twisted, and he covered his ears with his knees. "Sure, whatever you say."

The hermit kept babbling. "Crunch, crunch, crunch! Crunch, crunch, crunch! Crunch, crunch, crunch!"

2

Endlessly, the hermit blathered, turning his threatening musings into a jingle of sorts.

With the hermit's commotion in the background, Dyphestive said to Grey Cloak, "You're the thief. Can't you pick the locks? You said you could escape from anything."

Grey Cloak lifted his head and said, "My tools are in my cloak. Do you see my cloak?"

Dyphestive scanned the cell. "No, but you said—"

"I know what I've said. Be quiet while I figure something out." He looked across the way. "Will you be *silent*?"

The hermit sang on. "Crunch, crunch, crunch. I like fingers. Crunch, crunch, crunch. I like toes. Crunch, crunch, crunch. I like the taste of little elf bones."

Grey Cloak shook his head. "Listen to me. First things

first. We need to get these chains out of the floor. I need you to break them."

Dyphestive held the chains in his huge hands and said, "I can't break these. They are too thick." His belly made a loud rumble. "And I'm hungry. You know I'm really weak when I'm hungry."

"Yes, you're weak like a hungry mule. Will you do it? We don't have time for excuses." He peered down the dungeon hall. "I think I hear someone coming."

Dyphestive scratched his messy sandy locks and said, "Even if I could break the chain, we still can't get through those steel bars."

"Nooo," Grey Cloak said with growing irritation, "but we would be free to fight our way out of here if need be."

With a nod, Dyphestive stood, braced his feet against the floor, and locked his hands around the chains. His tremendous shoulders knotted up, and the thick muscles in his bare arms bulged.

The hermit stopped singing and pressed his face against the bars. His eyes widened. "He's strong. I used to be strong like him once."

"Come on. You can do it. I know you can!" Grey Cloak said.

"I told you they are too thick." Dyphestive's face turned beet red, and he groaned.

"You aren't even trying. Try harder!" Grey Cloak yelled right in his friend's ear. "Pull!"

Dyphestive's face beaded with new sweat, and his arms shook.

"You can do it!"

The chain slackened. The large young man sat down with a loud gasp. "I can't do it." He panted. "I can't to it. I'm too hungry. It makes me weak."

Grey Cloak rolled his eyes. "Listen to me. We are going to die if you don't do this. Now is not the time to be a weakling."

Dyphestive arched an eyebrow. "I'm not a weakling. I'm a lot stronger than you."

"Yes, well, that goes without saying. You're an over-grown child. But even for a stripling of your size, you are surprisingly weak."

"I'm not weak." Dyphestive set his feet on the floor, wrapped the chains around his thick wrists, and started to pull. He grimaced from the strain and growled, and the metal links groaned.

Grey Cloak's eyes widened. "You can do it, weakling. Put your legs into it. Snap them."

Dyphestive's thighs and arms flexed as he heaved, and the metal chains snapped. His head hit the ceiling. "Ow."

"Quick, do mine," Grey Cloak said as he sawed his chain through the link. He put his right cuff against the floor ring. "Hurry!"

"I forgot to put my legs into it. I have it now." He locked his fingers around Grey Cloak's chain and wrenched the metal, his jaw clenching. The chains snapped.

"Told you," Grey Cloak said in a knowing fashion. He still had a metal wrist cuff on his right arm and a length of chain still attached, and he spun the chain around. "This might be useful."

Dyphestive gasped for breath and said, "You're welcome."

"We aren't out of here yet." Grey Cloak took a knee, ran his slender fingers up the leg of his trousers, and produced a small metal file that was sewn inside the leg of his pants. He stuffed the unique file into the cell's key lock.

"I thought you didn't have any tools," Dyphestive said.

"I always have tools."

"You are a thief!" the hermit said with a cackle.

"I'm an amateur adventurer."

"Ah, I see." The hermit clawed his long fingernails through his messy beard. "If you seek adventure, go to Jeddy. Find great fortune there. Red Claw Tavern. The freebooters thrive there. Steal a dragon. Save the world. Crunch, crunch, crunch."

"I can't wait to visit." Grey Cloak twisted the file deep inside the locking mechanism, and the lock popped. He shoved the barred door open and duck-walked out. "Let's go, Dyphestive."

Dyphestive hunched down and shoved his way through the opening. "I don't think these cells are made for people."

"They are made for smaller people, not oafs like you," the hermit said.

Dyphestive gave the hermit a funny look, and Grey Cloak glided down the slick floors of the dungeon. All of the cells he passed were empty, and the keys to the doors were hanging on a wooden peg beside the dungeon entrance. He pressed his ear to the door. Someone was snoring outside.

Grey Cloak grabbed a large set of pliers that was leaning against the wall. They were used to bolt the shackles on. He took them to Dyphestive. "Here."

Dyphestive used the pliers to twist the nuts off of Grey Cloak's shackles then started working on his.

"You are a strange pair. A human and an elf. A sharp-tongued elf and a dullard," the hermit said.

"We're blood brothers," Dyphestive said proudly.

The hermit's wild gaze slid back and forth between them. "Well, that's stupid."

Grey Cloak used the dungeon key on the old hermit's cell lock and pulled the door open. "Perhaps you should be more kind to your liberators. Come on now."

The hermit shut himself back inside the cell.

"What are you doing?" Grey Cloak opened the door again. "Let's go."

"I didn't ask you to free me. Leave me alone!" The hermit shut himself inside again. "I don't like you or you.

And I didn't say that you could leave, either." He shouted at the top of his lungs, "Guards! Guards! Guards!"

Grey Cloak exchanged a dumbfounded look with Dyphestive. Angry voices came from the other side of the dungeon entrance, and a key was shoved in the lock. Their jailers were coming.

3

GREY CLOAK STOLE DOWN THE CORRIDOR AND HID behind the dungeon door just as it opened. A trio of kobolds slipped inside with their spears thrust forward. The kobolds were ugly humanoids standing just over four feet tall, with fox-shaped faces covered with scaly skin instead of fur.

"Guards! Guards!" the hermit shrieked. He pointed and shook a finger at Dyphestive, who was standing stock-still. "He's escaping! There is an elf on the loose too!"

Dyphestive charged down the hall with his open hands in front of him. "Come and get me!"

Three more kobolds entered the dungeon, making six in all. As soon as the last one passed by the door, Grey Cloak tripped him. The kobold fell forward, knocking the pack down like dominoes, but the one in the front skipped away from his falling brood. He lowered his spear and charged Dyphestive, gnashing his sharp teeth.

Dyphestive's broad body filled the cramped corridor. He grabbed the spear by the shaft and ripped it out of the kobold's clawed fingers. "It's like taking a wooden sword from a child. How'd they get the drop on us anyway?" He reached for the kobold.

The kobold ducked underneath Dyphestive's arms, latched onto his leg, and sank his teeth into his knee.

"Ouch. Stop biting me, you devilish hound."

"Will you quit playing with that thing? We need to get out of here!" Grey Cloak said as he skipped away from a jabbing spear.

The quick little men scrambled to their feet and attacked Grey Cloak with savagery, but he sidestepped and jumped away from the spear thrusts. He grabbed one spear from an attacker and used it to block the attack of another then planted a heel in a kobold's jaw and boxed another one's ears. "Will you *hurry?*" he shouted.

Dyphestive wrenched the kobold free from his leg then lifted the writhing figure over his head and whistled loudly.

The fierce knot of guards turned toward the sound just as Dyphestive hurled the kobold like a hay bale into them. The entire pack was knocked to the ground. Dyphestive bounded past them and headed up the short flight of steps to the landing where Grey Cloak was waiting by the door.

Grey Cloak shoved his friend through. "Keep moving, you big ox. What did you want to do—paint a picture?"

The moment Grey Cloak passed the threshold, he slammed the door behind them, latched the lock, and dropped the door bar. Small fists began beating the door. Panting, he leaned against the door with a satisfied smile and said, "Well done, brother."

Dyphestive dabbed his forehead with his wool vest and said, "He bit me. The stinking little thing bit me."

"You'll live. Come on."

Grey Cloak led the way through a sandstone corridor that gently sloped upward. At the end of the corridor was a small set of stairs leading up to the open sky. The sun was hidden behind the heavy rain clouds that were releasing a steady drizzle, and Dyphestive caught some raindrops in his mouth.

"Will you stop that?"

"I'm thirsty, Grey."

Grey Cloak shook his head. "Yes, of course you are. And hungry. And weak." He eyeballed his surroundings. The kobold community consisted of huts made from wood and had animals scattered all over a sparsely vegetated, hard-packed dirt terrain. Grey Cloak knew exactly where they were. It was Farhook, and he was exactly where he'd planned to be.

Dyphestive pinched his nose. "You certainly pick the worst-smelling places to rob. There's nothing worse than the oily-salty-manure-type smell of gnolls and kobolds. Perhaps it's time you took up another profession."

"I don't think so."

Scores of kobolds were milling through the village, laboring at huge bonfires, and chasing wild chickens. Grey Cloak and Dyphestive ducked down into the dungeon pit as two burly gnolls walked by. The gnolls were a beastly race, built like men, with wolflike faces, short dog snouts, and necks like bulls. The passing pair wore piecemeal armor and carried iron swords on their hips.

As the gnolls moved farther away, Dyphestive crinkled his nose and said, "I told you they stink."

"Yes, your observation is brilliant." Grey Cloak scanned the area. Gnoll men and women towered over the kobolds that served at their beck and call. It looked like a feast was being prepared near one of the bonfires. He pointed. "There!"

"What?"

"My cloak."

"My boots," Dyphestive added. "Ew, that gnoll is wearing them. I'm never going to get them back."

"Oh, we're getting them back. We're getting everything back." Grey Cloak clenched his jaw at the sight of the gnoll wearing his cloak like a scarf over his brawny shoulders. "It looks ridiculous on him."

Dyphestive put a heavy hand on Grey Cloak's shoulders and said, "We need to part with them. No cloak or boots is worth this."

Grey Cloak brushed his blood brother's hand aside and said, "I didn't come to be taken. I came to take. They are the same goat and cattle snatchers that we've been dealing with. We are going to take back what is ours and then some, just like I planned."

"What do you mean?"

When Grey Cloak spied the largest hut in the area, he guessed that it was where the gnoll tribe leader lived. "I bet his treasure is in there."

"I thought we came to take back our flock."

"And some additional spoils." He looked from side to side. "We need a distraction."

"You're going to get us caught again."

"I didn't get us caught. *You* did." He drummed his finger on his chin. "Now, let me see." He spied the livestock corral, which held horses, goats, pigs, and sheep.

As they watched, the gnolls and kobolds started to don crude ceremonial garb made from blood-dipped feathers and bones that they used to decorate their headdresses and began wild dances and singing. They changed at a large totem pole with different painted dragonheads. The tribes began to cluster.

"Now's our chance," Grey Cloak said. "You go over to the horse pen and start letting them out."

Dyphestive frowned. "What are *you* going to do?"

"I'm going into that tent. I didn't come all this way for nothing." He glanced up. The rain started to come down harder. "Perfect."

"We should run for it," Dyphestive warned.

"Don't worry. I have it all under control. Follow me." With Dyphestive in tow, Grey Cloak raced into a hut he'd seen the tribe coming out of earlier, wearing the ceremonial dress. All sorts of robes and animal skins and bones littered the floor, and he began suiting up in the garb.

Dyphestive held up a bearskin and dropped it over his shoulders then added a wooden mask carved like a boar's head. "How does this look?"

"Hideous. It will be perfect. Now, go let the livestock out. Send the horses one way and the sheep and goats back toward the Iron Hills." He donned a robe covered with sewn-in animal bones.

A wild cry went up outside, and they peeked through the door. Gnolls and kobolds had clustered at the underground dungeon entrance.

The gnoll leader, the biggest of them all, bellowed in a vicious voice, "Find them! Find our dinner now!"

4

"Under no circumstances is this a reason to panic," Grey Cloak said as he dropped a mask that looked like a chicken over his head. "Act like you belong. It should be easier for you because you are built like one of them."

"Ha-ha." Dyphestive took another peek outside. "What are you going to do?"

"You let loose the horses. I'll go steal the loot."

"What loot?"

Grey Cloak shook his chicken head. "This tribe is a bunch of looters. Not only do they cross the Iron Hills to steal livestock, but they raid caravans as well. You saw the weapons they carry. They are a well-armed force when they are full in number."

"So you are going to steal from them and give it back to the people they stole it from."

"Uh... perhaps." He started pushing Dyphestive toward the door. "Go on now. Act like a two-legged boar. Blend in."

"But..."

Grey Cloak didn't stick around to listen to Dyphestive's objections. He dashed through the village, pretending he was looking for escaped prisoners. A pair of kobolds rushed right by him without giving him so much as a glance, making him chuckle. *What a stupid bunch of people.*

He angled toward the largest hut in the camp. It was big enough for a dozen gnolls to sleep in. Pushing aside the blanket that was used for a door, he found the inside of it empty. The furnishings were sparse. Animal furs were scattered over the floor along with a few small storage chests and clayware with scraps of old food. He tapped his fingertips together. *Perfect.*

One by one, Grey Cloak opened the chests. He found worthless jewelry made out of river rocks along with fine linens, spices in jars, and silver tableware. The craftsmanship of the items made it clear that they weren't made by gnolls or goblins but looked like something fashioned by men. He rummaged through all three chests but found nothing of value or interest.

"Sad. Plain sad. There has to be something more valuable than this." He picked up a silver tinderbox. "Couldn't you at least be gold? That would be worth something." He dug deeper into the chest. "Worthless. Worthless. Worthless."

Outside, a gnoll started barking orders. "Check every hut! Now! Now! I'll check mine."

Grey Cloak closed the lid of the chest and dove underneath the fur blankets. He flattened himself beneath the pile, closed his eyes, breathed softly, and listened.

Heavy footsteps entered the hut accompanied by heavy breathing. The gnoll that entered the room took deep draws into his nose. Bones from a necklace rattled as he walked around. A thumb scraped over the edge of a blade. "Hmm," the gnoll growled in his throat.

The gnoll lifted a chest and set it aside, making the contents rattle, then he grunted again, and it sounded like he was setting the chest back in its original place. The loud sniffing started again, and the strange grunt followed.

"I smell something," he said in a raspy voice. "Something rotten." The gnoll started lifting blankets off of the floor and tossing them aside. "Where are you, rodent?" He pulled up another blanket. "Where are you, juicy meat?"

Slowly, the blankets were lifted from the pile on top of Grey Cloak. "Hmm... looks lumpy," the gnoll said.

The edge of a sword began to trace over Grey Cloak's body. Only two fur blankets were left on top of him. He couldn't help but swallow underneath the suffocating mess. *Please go away! Please go away!*

The gnoll snorted again and started to gently poke the furs with the tip of his sword. *"Mim moe culla doe.* A thief smells a thief. But this thief will feast on elf bones." He tapped the blade harder on the blankets. "If you are in there, you better come out." He poked the blankets again. "I count. Then I gore. One. Two..."

5

SLIPPING INTO THE FRENZIED CROWD, DYPHESTIVE made his way toward the animal pens. He crouched behind the wooden rails that made up the split fencing. The sheep were bleating, and he reached into the pen to pet one of them. Stroking the wool, he said, "Don't worry, little one. I'll take you home."

More sheep moved toward the call of his voice, and they started nuzzling his hands and face through the fence. "Yes, yes, I missed you too. I'll be back."

Dyphestive duck-walked toward the horse stables, where numerous steeds were inside a large pen. He began sliding the railing away, opening the section of the pen like a gate, and crept inside. A black stallion stood in the midst of the team of horses, towering above the rest. He smacked it hard on the rear and said, "Eeyah!"

The great stallion bolted out of the gap in the pen, and over a score of horses galloped after their leader.

He smiled inside and nodded. "Another task well done." Flailing his arms wildly, he ran after the horses. The tribe of gnolls and kobolds played right into his hands. They dashed after the horses at full speed. He watched them pass him, subtly veered away, and headed back to the animal pens.

TENSED UNDERNEATH THE BLANKETS, Grey Cloak was a moment from giving himself up when a call came from outside.

"The horses! The prisoners steal away on the horses!" another gnoll yelled from the hut's doorway.

"What?" The gnoll leader stormed out of the hut.

Grey Cloak's eyes brightened as he lifted the blankets. The hut was void of any humanoids, but gnolls and kobolds were shouting outside. "Well done, Dyphestive, well done," he muttered.

He headed straight for the chest that the gnoll had moved and shoved it aside. Underneath the chest was a small blanket that he tossed away. A small, crudely crafted wooden box, big enough for a pair of boots, rested inside.

"Well, what do we have here." Grey Cloak opened the lid to the box. "Golden apples, I found the booty."

Inside the box was a burgundy pouch made of crushed velvet. He untied the purse strings and dumped the contents in his hand. Small gemstones and several pieces of gold called chips glinted in his palms. He rolled one of the golden coins between his knuckles. With a grin, he said, "I like it."

Grey Cloak spied another object lying in the box. It was a dagger in a well-crafted black sheath. He pulled the dagger from the sheath and thumbed the edge. The keen blade drew blood. It had an onyx handle, and the pommel and small crossguard were gilded in fine silver. Though it was razor sharp, he wasn't sure if it was a ceremonial dagger or if it was fully functional. He flipped it in his hand. It had a very good balance. "This haul keeps getting better."

He sheathed the dagger and put it in the back of his pants then tied the pouch to his belt and shoved the chest back into place. Patting himself on the back, he said, "Well done, if I don't mind saying so myself." He headed toward the flap.

DYPHESTIVE BEGAN FREEING the sheep and goats from the pen. "Come," he said to the goats, "come."

The goats remained content chewing the nubs of grasses, while the sheep began to filter out.

"Stubborn," he said. He felt a tap on his shoulder. He

stood up and turned around. "It's about time you stopped fooling around, Grey." Then he gawped as he stood face to face with a gnoll.

The gnoll leader was much taller than Dyphestive and had hairy arms knotted with muscles leading up to his heaving neck and shoulders. Grey Cloak's cloak was draped over the hound-headed man's shoulders. With both hands, the gnoll lifted Dyphestive's mask off of his head.

"Hello," Dyphestive said with a goofy smile.

The gnoll's lips curled back over his canine teeth. "I will dine on your bones, human stripling!" He tossed his head back and let out a wild howl.

Dyphestive drew back a fist and punched the gnoll in the gut with all that he could, and the breath exploded out of the gnoll's mouth. He doubled over, clutching his belly. Like a hammer driving a nail, Dyphestive dropped both of his fists down on the gnoll's back, making the gnoll drop to a knee.

He raised his fists again, but with animal savagery, the gnoll twisted his body toward Dyphestive and struck him in the chest. The hard blow knocked Dyphestive backward, and the gnoll charged and tackled him.

Dyphestive rolled over the muddy ground with the gnoll, and the gnoll's slavering jaws dripped as he bit at Dyphestive's neck. He planted his strong fingers around the gnoll's neck and squeezed with all of his might. "Get off of me!"

The gnoll responded in kind by locking its iron grip around Dyphestive's throat, and they rolled over the ground, with one topping the other back and forth. Though Dyphestive squeezed so hard his fingers ached, the gnoll's animal strength did not yield. His sharp fingernails dug into the skin of Dyphestive's neck. "Now, you will die."

With his air supply cut off, doubt began to creep into Dyphestive's mind. *He gets stronger. I get weaker. I don't want to die!*

6

CHOKING TO DEATH, DYPHESTIVE TAPPED INTO THE reserves of strength that churned within him. He gave it all he had, and his immense hands began to crush the cords of sinew in the gnoll's broad neck. The gnoll's eyes popped in their sockets. He started to flail and squirm, and his grip slackened. Dyphestive rolled on top of the dying gnoll and gave a final flex of his arms and hands. The gnoll let out a dying gasp and shuddered one last time.

Panting, Dyphestive rolled away and lay on his back, looking up at the raindrops falling from the sky. When Grey Cloak appeared, he asked, "Where have you been?"

Grey Cloak patted his purse and said, "Making us rich." He scanned the area. "They'll be coming back soon. Let's move on. Quickly."

Dyphestive rolled up to his seat and started pulling his

boots off of the gnoll. While he did that, Grey Cloak retrieved his cloak.

"I hated to kill him," Dyphestive said.

"Would you rather he killed you?" Grey Cloak donned his cloak and frowned. "It's all muddy."

"We came to get the flock, not kill." He began tugging his boots on.

"Don't be a fool. These gnolls are natural-born killers. They have more blood on their hands than we would ever want to imagine." Grey Cloak pointed at the village. "Look around. Do you see any women or children? This is a haven for brigands. Nothing else."

Dyphestive stood up and called to the sheep, who came, but the goats didn't budge.

"The sheep know our voice, but the goats refuse to listen." Grey Cloak chuckled. "Let's save the ones we can." He grabbed a stick and started prodding the sheep along.

Cradling a small sheep in his arms, Dyphestive started walking westward toward the Iron Hills and the narrow passage that snaked through them. They had traveled at a brisk pace with the flock for almost a league when a clamor of angry voices called up the channel.

They stopped and looked back. The gnolls and kobolds were tracking them down, and it sounded like all of them.

"We're never going to make it with these sheep," Grey Cloak said. "We must run. Leave the sheep."

"I'm not leaving them," Dyphestive replied. He

scanned the rocky ledges. "You go ahead. Lead the sheep. I have an idea."

"You have an idea?" Grey Cloak smirked.

"Go on, will you." Dyphestive climbed the jagged rocks of the channel and up a steep incline. His fingers found purchase on the jagged rocks that led higher up into the hills. From his vantage point, he could see Grey Cloak leading the sheep through the channel at an agonizingly slow pace. The gnolls and kobolds were racing up the passage in droves. "This will be close."

He found a boulder bigger than he was feebly wedged between two pine trees and put his back against it and started to push, but the rock didn't budge. "Barnacles." He planted the heels of his boots against a tree root jutting out of the ground. "Remember, use your legs." He clenched his jaw. "Hurk!" His thick thigh muscles strained the seams of his trousers, the oblong boulder started to shift, and the bark on the trees cracked.

Dyphestive started to rock the boulder. It budged little by little, and bits of debris mixed with pine needles began rolling down the hill. He put all of his leg and back strength into it and pushed harder, and the boulder broke free of its prison and tumbled down the hill.

"Yes!" he said as he stumbled backward and fell awkwardly down the hill. He watched in amazement as the boulder crashed down the rocky hillside, busting more rocks on the way down, creating an avalanche.

The clamor of the falling boulder caused the wild-eyed gnoll tribe to stop in their tracks and look up in horror. They scrambled down the passage as the rocks and dirt began to fill it like an empty grave. Many gnolls and kobolds escaped, but others were crushed and buried. The survivors fled.

Dyphestive strolled down the slippery hill with a smile on his face and wiped his muddy hands on his trousers. He caught up with his friend.

"Well, that was well done," Grey Cloak said.

"I couldn't have done it without my boots." Dyphestive lifted his leg and wiggled his boot around, but then he stopped.

"What's wrong?"

"I just noticed... they feel all squishy inside."

"That's probably because the gnoll that wore them left something growing in them."

"Ew!" Dyphestive hopped around and yanked his boots off.

Laughing, Grey Cloak led the sheep away.

7 IRON HILLS

Having slept into the wee hours of the dark morning, Grey Cloak suddenly woke. He sat up and rubbed his bleary eyes. A pine tree was at his back, and he'd been wrapped up in his cloak. The crisp morning air was chilly, and the patches of grasses were dewy.

Dyphestive was snoring softly, curled up like a baby with his head resting on the back of a sheep like a pillow. At least a dozen sheep had formed a wall around him.

"Pitiful," Grey Cloak said as he yawned. He rubbed the fine hairs on the nape of his neck and realized the hair on his arms was upright. He quickly stood and pulled his new dagger from its sheath.

Shriek!

The alarming sound erupted in the gray clouds, which

lit up as if they had lightning churning within them. Another bone-chilling sound split the sky.

Shriek!

A dragon with a long-haired rider in full metal armor dropped out of the pillowy clouds. It was a tremendous beast with a hide of armored scales, a stout horn on its snout, and smoke and flames spilling from its mouth. Another dragon, just as big but darker, gave chase behind it.

"Oh my," Grey Cloak muttered. "Oh my. Sky Riders!"

The dragons chased one another like two enormous birds of prey with leathery wings beating like thunder. The second dragon had a larger person in blackened armor on it, firing arrows that streaked through the sky like glowing missiles. One of those arrows lodged itself in the lighter-scaled dragon's ribs, and the stricken dragon bucked.

With a yank of the reins, the long-haired rider turned the dragon back into the other dragon's path by doing an inverted loop then launched a glowing javelin downward at their attackers. It sliced through the air like lightning shot from the heavens and struck the dark dragon in the back between the wings. Light flashed; then came a thunderous explosion. *Boom!*

Grey Cloak shielded his eyes but could still see the man plummeting toward the ground. Chunks of wings, legs, and scales were raining down after him. The bodies hurtled into the rocky hills and hit with muted *thuds* behind them.

The surviving dragon and rider circled above their

victims, and the dragon let out a victorious shriek that turned into a roar. The winged lizard suddenly dipped in the sky. It began to spiral with one of its wings hanging limp. It came right at Grey Cloak's location on the crest of the hill and dropped out of sight behind the hills less than a league away.

Grey Cloak hustled over to Dyphestive and shook him. "Did you hear that? Sky Riders. Wake up!"

Dyphestive balled up tighter, so Grey Cloak kicked his brother, turned, jumped the sheep that were clustered at his feet, and headed after the fallen dragon.

In the night, with the wind whistling in his ears, Grey Cloak ran like a deer, the liberating feeling of being able to move at full speed bringing him sheer delight. Traveling with others was like moving with anchors on his legs. When he was alone, no one could catch him.

He weaved through the trees and over the dips of the rugged terrain with the surefootedness of a mountain goat and the speed of a mountain cat. Without breaking stride, he ducked under branches and hopped over small channels and cracks in the terrain. In a short amount of time, he covered the distance between where he started and where he thought the dragon rider had landed. He wasn't even breathing heavily when he got there.

Aside from the pine trees that were scattered over the Iron Hills, the terrain was barren and rugged. Rocks would slip underfoot, and the sudden climbs were steep. He made a silent trek through the area and combed his hair back over his pointed ear to listen.

Grey Cloak crouched down and squinted. Slowly, he looked from side to side, running his gaze over the hard ground. The terrain was lumpy all over. Any one of the dark rock formations could be a dragon. *The beast was wounded. Certainly there should be some stirrings. Or blood?*

A rustling sound caught his ear. It was coming from a rise underneath a rocky cliff. On cat's feet, he walked toward it, climbed up the hump in the ground, and looked down on the gap underneath. Before his vision focused on the stirrings in the shadows of the gap, a dagger blade was pushed against his neck.

8

"REMAIN PERFECTLY STILL OR DIE," A WOMAN SAID AS she pushed the flat of her dagger blade harder against Grey Cloak's neck.

Barnacles! He couldn't believe someone had gotten the drop on him. *How did I miss her?* A full suit of armor brushed against his body. The woman's grip was very strong. He swallowed and said, "I was only... *ulp*... curious."

"Curiosity will get you killed, elf," she said. Using her free hand, she put him in a headlock and held tight. "Who else is with you?"

Grey Cloak was honest, but he played dumb. "Er... just my brother. He is sleeping. With the sheep. Your battle in the heavens woke me."

"You're a shepherd?"

He lifted his foot and wiggled his toes. He'd never found his boots in Farhook. "As poor as a pauper."

The woman patted him down.

"This is a little uncomfortable," he said. "I mean, I don't even know your name."

"Don't flatter yourself, stripling." She let him loose and held his dagger in one hand and his coin purse in the other. "Poor, you say." She dumped the coins and the small gems onto the ground. "My, they must be paying shepherds quite well these days. Perhaps I should change my trade."

"I found that."

"Sure, you did. Thieves are really good at finding things, aren't they." She flipped his dagger in the air and let it drop point first in a rock at her feet. Her bright eyes widened. "That's quite a blade you carry. Where did you get it?"

Grey Cloak took his first really full look at the woman. She was very pretty, with tanned skin and a head of flowing red hair bleached by the sun. Her hands had calluses, and her plate-mail armor didn't make a sound when she moved. She was carrying a longsword and a dagger on her hips. A glance at the decorative pommels revealed that the weapons were of the highest craftsmanship. "What difference is that to you? It's mine. All of it, and it seems to me that you are robbing me, an innocent man, of his personal goods. Shame on you, Sky Rider. I thought your causes were noble."

Her eyes narrowed, and she approached him with a limp. "Listen to me, urchin. I will pull your tongue out of your mouth with my bare hands and feed it to you. You should show respect. In these wild hills, I'm well within my reason to kill you."

"That sounds like something a crazy person would say," he quipped. He was about to say something else but stayed silent when a great shadow appeared over him, and hot, steamy breath came down over his body, instantly dampening his long hair and his clothing. He looked up at a mouthful of huge sharp teeth.

"And if she doesn't kill you, perhaps I will," the dragon said coolly. His head was as big as a cow, and his hot breath curled the hair on Grey Cloak's arms. "And I'm very hungry. I've never eaten an elf before, but did someone say something about sheep?"

"This elf claims to be a shepherd," she said. "But he's lying. He's only a common thief."

"No, I'm not lying," he answered quickly. "I really am a shepherd, and I really do have sheep."

"How many sheep?" the dragon asked. "I'm really hungry, Anya."

Anya glared at the dragon. "Will you be silent?"

"That's a pretty name," Grey Cloak said. He could see in her face that him knowing her name bothered her. "It's nice to meet you. I'm Grey Cloak."

With her hands on her hips, Anya laughed. "You're named after a garment. What a silly little elf."

"It's an adventurer's name."

"It's a thief's name."

The dragon groaned and said, "As long as we are talking about names, my name is Cinder. And I'm very hungry, not to mention wounded." He swung his large head toward Anya. "You know how I get when I am hungry and wounded. That arrow in my side burned like fire."

"I pulled the arrow out. You're fine," Anya said.

Cinder bent his neck down and sniffed Grey Cloak, who was still sitting in front of the jagged rise. "He smells of sheep." His huge tongue licked his sharp rows of front teeth. "Ah, delicious little sheep. How many, elf?"

"Cinder," Anya said, "we need to go. You can feast later. We have more important matters to attend to. We need to dispose of the Risker."

The dragon rolled his eyes. He lifted his wing in an awkward fashion and said, "I can't fly like this. Not without food."

"You sound like my brother," Grey Cloak quipped.

The dragon lifted his massive body out of the crevice that he was nestled in. He was much larger than he'd appeared in the sky. Warmth emanated from his body. He walked away on all fours, dragging a tail behind him that was as mighty as a cedar.

"Come back, Cinder! Come back now!" Anya gave a frustrated growl. "He's impossible to deal with when he's hungry."

Grey Cloak quietly stood and said, "I know that feeling." He bent over to grab his dagger, which was still stuck in the hunk of rock.

Anya snaked her sword out quicker than a blink and held the tip at his neck. "What do you think you are doing?"

He froze in place and said, "You are very fast. I didn't even see that. Uh, I was only retrieving my belongings. You must know that it would be foolish of me to trifle with a Sky Rider as mighty as you."

"You are well spoken for a youth. Where were you raised?" She lifted his chin with the edge of her sword.

Raising his hands, he said, "Havenstock. I live in Havenstock." He wiggled his fingers. "Please don't kill me."

She sheathed her sword. "I wouldn't kill a stripling, even an ogre stripling. Even though I probably should." Her gaze followed Cinder's trail, and she marched in that direction.

Grey Cloak gathered his belongings and fell in step behind her.

DYPHESTIVE STIRRED from his slumber and slowly sat up. He had chill bumps all over his body. The sheep, which had shielded him from the wind, were gone. He rubbed his bare arms. All was deathly quiet aside from a loud crunching sound. He twisted around and jumped backward. "Goy!" His heart shot into his throat.

A huge dragon was seated many yards behind him. Using his huge clawed hands, the dragon stuffed sheep into his mouth one by one then chewed them up and swallowed them with big gulping sounds.

Dyphestive grabbed a stone and hurled it at the dragon. The rock bounced off of the dragon's snout, and the dragon scooped up another sheep and stuffed it into his great jaws.

"Stop eating my sheep!" Dyphestive shouted.

The dragon ignored him and swept up another sheep and ate it. Only one sheep was left, a lamb that was only a few weeks old. Without thinking, Dyphestive dashed toward his lamb.

The dragon's eyes followed him like a cat tracking a mouse. His tail lashed out, caught Dyphestive's legs, and sent him tumbling through the air.

He landed hard and off balance. "Oof!" He rolled up to his knees and scrambled after the lamb, but the dragon's tail slammed down, cutting off his path to the sheep. Dyphestive hurdled over the tail, but it snapped upward and flipped him through the air.

"Guh!" Dyphestive rolled onto his back. The dragon's large tail was pinning him to the ground. He pushed at it, but it didn't budge.

The dragon leaned over him. Hot breath came from his mouth, and his nostrils huffed out rings of smoke. "All of this effort over a little lamb," he said. "I'm impressed. Only a good shepherd would dare tangle with a dragon." The dragon grinned. "You are a meaty one. Three or four sheep in one. You'll make a fine dessert." He opened his jaw as wide as a tunnel.

"Cinder! Stop!"

Dyphestive turned toward the source of the voice, and a human woman of striking beauty caught his eye. He momentarily forgot about the dragon's tail crushing his chest. His heart was captivated.

"Stop what, Anya?" the dragon, Cinder, said innocently.

"You know what." Anya was wearing a well-fashioned suit of plate-mail armor and walked with a slight limp. "Don't eat that man."

Cinder lifted his tail. "When will I ever complete a full-course meal?" He eyed the lamb. "That's not even a morsel." He scooted the lamb over to Dyphestive with his tail. "You can eat it."

Dyphestive scooped the lamb into his arms and stood up. He hadn't taken his eyes off of Anya. Grey Cloak stepped into his line of view, and he tried to look past him.

"Glad to see that you are well, brother," Grey Cloak said. He patted Dyphestive on his back then turned toward Anya. "I told you we were shepherds."

"Yes." Anya stepped forward. "And this is your *brother*? A human?"

"We're blood brothers," Dyphestive said brightly. With

the lamb still in his arms, he stuck out his hand. "I'm Dyphestive."

Anya walked by him and faced her dragon. "It's time that we were moving along. I see your belly is bulging, and your wing doesn't appear to be so broken."

Cinder flexed his wings and gently flapped them. "I can manage." He lowered himself to the ground.

Anya climbed onto the dragon's saddle, which was made of leather and had oversized quivers that held javelins and spears. She leaned over, grabbed an open-faced helm that was fashioned like a dragon's face on the top, and put it on. Cinder rose.

"Grey Cloak. Dyphestive. Stay out of trouble." She looked up at the sky and tugged the reins. "Upward, Cinder. Upward!"

Cinder used his powerful hind legs to launch into the air. His wings beat, creating a strong wind. Higher and higher they went until they shot off into the early-morning horizon and disappeared in the clouds.

"She knows my name," Dyphestive said in a heartfelt voice.

Grey Cloak slapped him in the shoulder. "How can you be smitten with her? She's over half again your age, probably older. But I'm certain that she did take a shine to me."

"Did not," Dyphestive said.

"Did too—we had a very long conversation, the Sky Rider and me. Her eyes were fastened on me."

"Sky Rider, huh," Dyphestive said as he gazed to the sky. "I'm going to marry a Sky Rider."

"Don't be silly. Get your head out of the clouds. You're only a shepherd."

Dyphestive lowered his gaze and scanned the rugged terrain. "My sheep! That dragon ate all of our sheep. Rhonna is going to kill us!"

9

"IT'S BEEN QUITE A TREK," GREY CLOAK SAID. THEY were walking on a dirt road that led west toward Havenstock. Sprawling grassland stretched north and west as far as the eye could see. They'd escaped the Iron Hills over a day ago and still had over a day of travel on foot left to go. With the warm sun on his face, he couldn't help but smile as he patted his pouch full of treasure. "But it's been worth it."

Dyphestive lumbered along with the lamb tucked in his arms. "Half of those spoils are mine."

"Half? Pfft, I don't see how you are coming up with half. You didn't do anything. Besides, you didn't want to steal it in the first place. I found it. Finders keepers."

"That's not right," Dyphestive replied glumly. "Besides, we were only supposed to recover the stolen flock."

"True, but I saw an opportunity and seized it. If you'd suggested the same, I would gladly support your half, but given the circumstances, I can only offer a tenth."

"I'll tell Rhonna."

"Erg. Fine, a quarter."

"I'll take a quarter and the dagger," Dyphestive said.

Grey Cloak gave an offended look. "The dagger? Now, why would one such as you need a dagger? You are as strong as an ox. Look at me—skin and bones. I don't have the wherewithal to defend myself without a weapon. But if I had half of your *colossal* strength, well, I would give you my dagger. I would give you everything."

Dyphestive made a dopey smile, nodded, and said, "I see your point. But you shouldn't try to short me. I'm your blood brother. You shouldn't do family like that."

"Don't you think we are getting too old for silly bonds? We'll be men soon, and we were very young when we made that pact."

Slack-jawed, Dyphestive stopped in his tracks, then he gathered himself and said with a hurt look, "But we made a bond. My word is my word. I have nothing else."

Grey Cloak's chest tightened. His brother's words tugged at his heart. The two of them had been together as long as he could remember. He put his hand on his brother's back and pushed him along. "Oh, don't get all sappy on me. I'm not going anywhere. Besides, you are the one that wanted to run off and get married. Where would that have left me? I would have been standing all alone while you rode off on a dragon, with your very old, old bride."

Dyphestive chortled. "She's not that old."

"She must have been one hundred."

THE NEXT MORNING, Grey Cloak and Dyphestive came across a covered wagon that was stuck in a huge rut in the road. The wagon was pulled by a single horse.

A young and pretty half elf with short auburn hair waved them down. "Can you help me? Please?"

"Certainly," Grey Cloak offered. He inspected the young woman as well as the wagon. She was wearing a blue skirt and white blouse and had a twinkle in her warm green eyes. Kneeling, he said with a dashing smile, "It shouldn't be a problem. All you need is a lift. It looks like your horse is too old to pull it out. Uh, are you traveling alone?"

"No, I am with my grandmother. She is very sick. I'm taking her to Raven Cliff to see a healer," she said. She squatted down beside Grey Cloak and extended her hand. "My name is Zora."

He squeezed her warm palm. "Grey Cloak." He tipped his chin toward his brother. "That's Dyphestive."

She smiled at Dyphestive. "Hello. I'm thankful for your arrival. You couldn't have shown up at a better time. No one has passed for hours, and I don't like being so close to the

Iron Hills." She looked south, where the Iron Hills were leagues distant. "They give me the shivers."

"You'll be safe," he assured her. "We'll have you moving in no time at all. Dyphestive, do you think you can help her out?"

"I can try." Dyphestive put his lamb down and hopped down into the wide and deep rut. The wagon had veered off the road, and the back wheel was half deep in the seam. He squatted down, secured his hands underneath the back of the wagon, and started to push up. The entire back end of the wagon lifted.

Zora hurried over to her horse while saying, "My, he's strong!" She walked the horse forward, and the wagon wheel eased its way back onto the road. "You made that look so easy."

Dyphestive dusted his hands off and said, "It was."

Zora gave him a big hug and said thanks then moved over to Grey Cloak, wrapped her arms around him, and kissed him repeatedly on the cheek. "Thank you, thank you, thank you!" She climbed back into the wagon. "I hate to rush, but I am worried about my grandmother. I must make haste. But thank you again, sweet young men. If you are ever in Raven Cliff, look for me." She snapped the reins and waved wildly. "Goodbye, now! Goodbye!"

The horse and wagon sped away, making a cloud of dust behind them.

"That horse is faster than it looked," Dyphestive said.

Grey Cloak was rubbing his cheek. "Huh? Oh, yes, it is fast. She was very pretty, don't you think?"

Dyphestive nodded.

The rest of the day, Grey Cloak walked with a spring in his step, and he was all smiles as they made camp that night. He lay on his cloak, looking up at the stars, while Dyphestive warmed his hands over the campfire.

"I think I will travel to Raven Cliff and see how Zora's grandmother fared," he said. "Wouldn't that be the polite thing to do?"

Dyphestive broke some sticks and dropped them onto the fire. "I suppose. It sounds like you are smitten."

"Pfft. I'm not smitten. Just... curious."

"Well, you have a small fortune to spend on her. Maybe you could buy her a new horse for her wagon."

"I bet she would like flowers from Agathan. I hear they have the most incredible gardens in all of Gapoli. Perhaps a fur blanket for the winter. For her grandmother, not us, or her, I mean." Grey Cloak patted his waist. Then he sat upright, his eyes bigger than saucers.

Dyphestive asked, "What's wrong?"

"My pouch is gone!"

10 HAVENSTOCK

"Shepherds! You can't call yourself shepherds when you lose an entire flock!" Rhonna stomped her foot. She was a middle-aged dwarf with coal-black hair braided into a bun on top of her head. She wore a blacksmith's apron and shook a mallet in her stubby hand. "Yer the worst shepherds ever!" She slammed the mallet down on a work-table, marched over to the furnace, and stopped the bellows. The coals in the furnace glowed orange hot. "The only thing dumber than a shepherd is a sheep. But you are making a strong case for the sheep." She stuffed her hands into heavy leather gloves and pulled a rod of hot iron out of the furnace then started hammering it on a huge anvil. *Bang. Bang. Bang. Bang.* "There is something wrong with the pair of you."

"We didn't lose them all," Grey Cloak offered. He had a

small tack hammer and was gently hammering a belt buckle he'd made for himself. "We saved one lamb."

They were on the outskirts of Havenstock, among the endless farming fields that stretched out for leagues. Havenstock was a large town, with tens of thousands living in stone cottages spread throughout the rolling green hills.

Rhonna glared at him, her dark eyes as hard as diamonds. She waggled her hammer at him. "Don't you start with the fast talk. I'll have you working and sleeping in here for weeks."

Grey Cloak went back to his hammering. He hated working in the smithy. It was always hot and sticky, and sweat drenched his clothing all day long. Rhonna made him do it from time to time, knowing that he hated it. She said it would serve him well. He didn't agree.

"I told you that a dragon ate the flock. It's a true story."

"I don't care if Dyphestive ate them. The point is you lost them. All of them. Sheep and goats." Rhonna stormed through the smithy, swapping out tools and working on one project after another. Most of the metal works were farming equipment and horseshoes, but a few old axes and swords hung on the back wall. "Get to work!"

"I'm working!"

Rhonna stopped what she was doing, walked over to him, looked up, and said, "Did you raise your voice to me?"

"I was only shouting so that I could be heard over your working. This is a very loud place." He tapped on his belt buckle. "See, even my tinkering makes a lot of racket. I have to raise my voice to speak above it."

She pointed a stiff finger at the furnace. "Work the bellows. I need more heat."

Grey Cloak sighed and rolled his eyes. He slouched over to the bellows. On his knees, he pumped them gently with his hands.

"Harder. I need more heat than that," Rhonna said in a stiff voice that could crack a wall.

The more he pumped the bellows, the hotter the smithy became. New sweat beaded on his face. "If it gets any hotter, I'll be cooked alive," he muttered.

"What's that?"

"I said is it hot enough for you?"

She pushed a hunk of metal into the furnace. "No. Keep working."

With a grunt, he kept pumping. At first, working the bellows wasn't hard, but after several minutes, his back muscles started burning. That wasn't the only thing else burning, either. His temper had been on the rise ever since that half elf, Zora, robbed him. He'd insisted on going after her, but Dyphestive talked him out of it, reasoning that a good thief would have lied about her whereabouts. Reluctantly, Grey Cloak agreed, but only because he still had the dagger. *I'll find her one day.*

His arms tightened like bowstrings and began to ache, and large drops of sweat dripped off of his chin. A puddle formed between his knees. "Isn't this sort of work better suited for Dyphestive?" he groaned.

"If you could do what he could, I would make you pull plows too," she said.

"No," he said feebly and looked behind him. The open front of the forge overlooked leagues of farming fields. Dyphestive was in the middle of a muddy field. His large hands clawed at the rich dirt as he tugged a heavy plow behind him. "But I think he likes what he's doing."

Rhonna wiped her gritty hands on a rag and spied Dyphestive. She almost cracked a smile. "He's a glutton for punishment, that one."

"Then punish him, not me."

She grabbed him by the ear, gave it a twist and a tug, and said, "This is work, not punishment. I'm doing you a favor by strengthening your back and hardening your bones."

"It doesn't feel like a favor."

"You can't control your tongue, can you? Listen to me— you lost sheep and goats. Dozens of them. There are consequences for that."

"We tried to get them back."

"That was your first mistake. You aren't ready for that. You aren't seasoned men yet."

"I am a man," he argued.

"Wrong. You aren't a boy. You aren't a man. You are a stripling. You'll be a man the day you can move my anvil."

She pointed to an anvil that sat on a petrified log in the center of the forge. It must have weighed well over five hundred pounds. "Move that, and a man you'll be."

"Can *you* move it?" he asked.

She smacked him on the back of the head. "Who do you think put it there?" She dropped her dirty cloth over his head. "Now, go and hammer out some horseshoes. I'm going to eat."

11

THE SKY WAS FULL OF STARS, AND ANYA THE SKY RIDER
stared at their majesty. She lay against Cinder's body, his
scales as warm as morning biscuits. They were tucked away
in the mountains of Crow Valley. She began sharpening her
dagger with a stone.

"What is on your mind?" Cinder asked. His head was
resting on the ground, but he had his neck bent toward her.
"You seem... preoccupied."

"I'm curious about something," she said.

"Oh, and what might that be? Perhaps I can help."

"Those striplings we encountered at the Iron Hills... did
anything odd strike you about them?"

"The elf and the man?" He shook his head. "Nothing
comes to mind. The man did look more appetizing

compared to the elf. He had a lot of succulent meat on his bones. Why? Did you fancy them?"

Anya elbowed Cinder. "Of course not. They are practically children. But that isn't what I mean. Did it strike you as odd that they weren't terrified of you?"

Cinder snorted out a blast of smoke. "Humph. Now that you mention it, that *is* odd. Why, the very sight of me sends a mortal's skin fleeing from his bones. I do say, I feel slighted."

She pushed her hair out of her eyes. Thoughts of the brothers had been eating at her all day. At first, she tried to brush them off, but they stuck in her mind. She figured after the battle with the Risker, she was rattled. But both of the young men's faces kept popping up in her mind.

"Are you sure that you didn't detect anything *unique* about them?" she asked.

"What do you want from me? I was wounded and hungry. My mind was set on other things. Perhaps you should sleep on it."

"I can't sleep." Anya stood up and walked over to a smoldering pile of dragon bones. She and Cinder had fetched the bodies of the dragon and its rider and brought them to the mountain heights, and Cinder had used his dragon breath and turned the bodies to nothing but ash, scale, and bones. Her eyes were fixed on the smoldering embers, and she teared up. "Gustam and Evil Wing were formidable enemies. It could have been us smoldering in this pile."

"Yes, I am certain that Black Frost won't be very happy when he discovers that his brother has been killed," Cinder commented as he started to fall asleep. "The skies will be filled with terror."

"You say that lightly," she said.

"No, I take the war in the winds very seriously. And I would be lying if I didn't admit that I fear our days are numbered."

She kicked the ashes. "You and your bleak forecasts. We've had our share of victories. Many more will come. It is Black Frost that will be choking on his ashes one day."

"There is more fire in you than there is me. That is for certain." Cinder closed his eyes. "Come over here and rest. You're making me restless."

"You sleep. I'll stand guard," she said brusquely.

Moving through the mountains, she tried to clear her mind. She hadn't slept well in months, if not years. When she did sleep, it was restless. She climbed to the highest peak. The icy night winds howled through the peaks, creating a haunting moaning, and tore at her long blond hair.

She faced north. A thousand leagues away, Black Frost was plotting and scheming in Dark Mountain. He had only one mission in mind. *Slay the Sky Riders one and all.* They were the only hope for Gapoli, and very few were left.

Anya pulled her sword and stuck it tip first in the ground. She kneeled behind it and bowed. It was her father's sword. He had been a Sky Rider, and so had her mother. Black Frost killed them both. "Mother. Father. I swear the same oath I swear every day. I will avenge you."

12

It had been a long day. Evening came, and a bland dinner of cornmeal biscuits and a strip of ham had been served. Grey Cloak walked the farm alone. He was surrounded by fields of wheat and vegetables. The livestock pens were more numerous than he could count. Havenstock always stank of dirty animals.

He arched his back. "Argh."

Rhonna had busted his hump all the way up until he was served dinner. His hands ached from all of the hammering on the horseshoes he'd done. It was nothing more than one of her character-building drills that she preached about all the time.

He climbed onto a split-rail fence and sat down on the top post. He cast his eyes north, toward Portham. *Perhaps it's time for a change of scenery.* Being a shepherd and a farmer had proved to be more trying than he envisioned. He thought it would have been easy.

Lifting his chin, he said, "I can hear you, Dyphestive."

Dyphestive crept up behind him and shook the fence. "You did not."

"Of course I did. You breathe like an ox and walk like one too."

"I didn't hear anything."

Grey Cloak rolled his eyes. "Of course not."

Dyphestive joined him on the split-rail fence, and the wood railing groaned.

"You're going to break it, then I'll have to mend it," he said.

"It'll hold. I'm not that heavy."

"Said the bull a moment before the bridge gave way beneath him."

"What are you sulking about now?" Dyphestive asked. He whistled at a pony inside the pen, and the pony nickered and walked over to him, and he stroked its mane. "Are you mad that you lost our chips? If anyone should be mad, it should be me at you for losing them. But I'm not."

"I would feel more comfortable if you were. It makes me question your sanity that you aren't."

"We couldn't spend the gold, anyway. What would shepherds do with it? Buy new robes? Sandals. A horse. I thought we were being indu—uh..." Dyphestive scratched his temple.

"Discreet. Not indiscreet, just discreet," Grey Cloak replied. "Besides, I think it is time to move on. We've grown enough that I don't think anyone would recognize us now."

"You're only saying this because you want to chase that girl. Ruby."

"Zora was her name. And can you blame me? She stole my treasure. I *should* want to go fetch it."

Dyphestive patted the colt on the head and shooed it away. "I like Havenstock. It's been good here. I don't want to leave."

"Do you really want to sleep among the sheep and goats for the rest of your life? What sort of life is that?"

"I don't want to get caught and end up back in Dark Mountain. The things they will do to us." Dyphestive shook his head. "I like this plan. It's a good one. No one is going to search for us among abominable shepherds."

"I think you are too fond of livestock." He pulled his dagger out and tossed it in the air then deftly caught it with one hand and flipped it to the other. "But I am ready to leave. Plus, I want to see if this dagger is worth something. I can sell it and use the money for travel. Larger cities have special shops."

"You're going to Portham?"

"No. I thought about it, but I think I will go to Raven Cliff first."

"That's over a week away. You just want to chase that girl."

"No, I'm chasing adventure. Perhaps that hermit spoke the truth. We can find a company to join in Raven Cliff."

Dyphestive gaped at him. "You are going to take the word of a loon? That hermit was nothing but a babbler. I don't understand you. Why can't you be satisfied? You are always pushing for more."

"You don't have to come. You can stay here, be a farmer or shepherd, marry, have a litter of children, and live a happy life until you are old and gray."

"I don't want to get married. Not yet, at least." Dyphestive grabbed his brother's shoulder. "Where you go, I go, like it or not. We're—"

"Blood brothers. Yes, I know." Grey Cloak smiled. "I'm glad you've decided to come." He stood on the top post and stretched his arms out wide. "Won't it be exciting to spread our wings and fly? We are ready to see the entire world. All of Gapoli."

"Do you even know how big Gapoli is?"

"I know that we won't figure it out by sitting here."

"What?" Dyphestive said. "You want to leave now? Right now?"

"Why not? No one will miss us. Who would miss a shepherd? Bad shepherds at that."

Dyphestive shook his head. "I couldn't leave Rhonna without saying goodbye. She's been good to us."

"Pfft." Grey Cloak squatted down on the post. "Good to us? How do you figure? It is us that have been good to her. We've been free labor. She's never paid us so much as a piece of copper."

"She fed us and gave us a place to sleep."

"Yes, in the fields with the sheep or in the barns with the chickens. That's hardly what I call fair compensation."

Dyphestive made a look of concentration. "I never thought about it that way. But still, I'm not going to leave without saying goodbye."

"You got that right," someone said with a harsh voice that could shatter glass.

Grey Cloak and Dyphestive's heads snapped around.

Rhonna was standing behind them twenty steps away. A curled tobacco pipe hung from her mouth, and she huffed a stream of smoke.

"Uh, Rhonna!" Dyphestive jumped off of the fence and stood at attention.

Grey Cloak wanted to slap him. *How does she always creep up on me?* "We were only daydreaming, Rhonna. There is no reason to let your skull boil over it." He hopped to the ground and landed as gently as a cat.

"Sounds more to me like you were running away." She marched up to them and said, "Neither of you is going, anyway. You lost flocks of sheep and goats. You have to work it off, and that won't take months. It will take *years.*" She spied the dagger in Grey Cloak's hand. "What's this?"

He hid it behind his back. "Nothing."

"Hand it over!"

He gave her the dagger.

Her bushy black eyebrows lifted for a moment then furrowed, and she tucked the dagger into her blacksmith apron. "That might shave a year off. Now get to bed!"

13

SUNSHINE SCORCHED THE FIELDS IN A HEAT WAVE that lasted for weeks. Inside the forge, Grey Cloak wore his nimble fingers to the bone. New calluses built up on his palms. He didn't make a move without dripping sweat, and his jerkin remained soaking wet. He tossed another horseshoe in the bin. He must have made dozens of them. Wiping a rag across his brow, he asked Rhonna, "Can I go to the well and fetch a drink?"

Rhonna was replacing the spokes on a wagon wheel. She didn't look up.

"Please," he said.

"Make it quick," she replied.

He hustled out of the sweltering smithy, hoping to catch the morning breeze. Instead, he was met with stagnant heat and the sun glaring in his face. He shielded his eyes and headed for the well but stopped in his tracks.

Dyphestive was already hoisting a bucket of water out of the well hand over hand. He lifted the bucket to his lips and started gulping it down then poured the last of it all over his face and messy hair.

Grey Cloak approached and said, "Try to save some for the rest of us. There is a drought going on."

"Sorry." Dyphestive dropped the bucket into the well. "I'll fish you some out. How's it going today?"

Arching an eyebrow, Grey Cloak asked, "Are you really asking me that question, lummox?"

"I'm only being polite."

"Ask me again when we are on our way out of here."

Dyphestive rolled his eyes and said, "Not this again." He fished the bucket out of the well.

"As soon as I find my dagger, I'm gone." He took the bucket and drank. "Ahhh. With or without you."

"You're playing with fire."

"What? I can handle an old dwarf woman." He drummed his prominent chin with his fingers. "But I have to admit she is very good at hiding things. I've looked all over, and I can't find where she stowed it."

"I think you should leave well enough alone." Dyphestive squinted. A white carriage pulled by a team of black horses trotted down the road toward the forge. "Look at that wagon. It must be from Portham."

The four horses were fine beasts with shiny coats, and the wagon was alabaster white and trimmed with gold paint. Two hard-eyed knights were escorting the carriage. They wore chain mail armor underneath burgundy leather tunics and were well armed with swords and dirks on their belts. They had the shield of Portham sewn into their shoulders and rode tall in their saddles.

The tallest knight dropped out of his saddle. He had medium-length hair and a long moustache, and he marched over to the forge without giving Grey Cloak and Dyphestive so much as a glance.

Rhonna stepped out of the smithy, wiping her hands on a rag. She slung it over her shoulder. "What can I do for you?"

"My horse and one from the team have each thrown a shoe. I need them repaired immediately," the knight said in a demanding voice.

Rhonna nodded at the knight, tipped her head toward the smithy, and said, "Come inside."

Dyphestive and Grey Cloak exchanged a look.

"That's odd," Grey Cloak said. "She never lets anyone but us inside her forge."

The carriage door burst open and slammed hard into the side of the carriage. "Great dragons! It's suffocating in there!" A woman hopped out. She was wearing a fluffy green dress made from fine linen. Her hair was full of curls.

She fanned her face and practically staggered to the well, walking right between Grey Cloak and Dyphestive.

Exhausted, she leaned against the well and eyed the bucket in Grey Cloak's hands. She rolled her neck at him and said, "Well, water boy, get me some water before I collapse."

"Nelly! Nelly, darling! Get back inside the carriage." A heavyset bald man was hanging out of the carriage. He wiped his sweat-soaked face with a handkerchief. "You could get hurt out there."

Another woman stuck her head out. She had a really big nose and wore a powdered wig. "Don't you dare drink out of that bucket. It's not proper manners for a young lady."

"I'll be fine, Mother." Nelly shooed her parents away with her hand. She looked at Grey Cloak and said, "Parents. They are such a pain in the fanny."

"I wouldn't know," he replied as he handed her a bucket.

"Oh," Nelly said. She eyed the bucket and made a disgusted face. "Don't you have a ladle?"

He shook his head.

Nelly looked between them and said, "Well, fetch one."

Neither brother moved.

"Hurry!"

Dyphestive started to slide away.

Grey Cloak offered Nelly the bucket and said, "It will be fine. You can drink the same as the rest of us, can't you?"

Nelly looked him up and down and said, "I don't share the same trough as animals."

He stiffened. "Do I look like an animal to you? I'm an elf."

"An urchin is an urchin. And I shouldn't even be speaking to you, or you, me." She looked at Dyphestive. "What are you waiting for, ogre? Fetch me a ladle. Fetch it now."

"Yes, ma'am." Dyphestive started to back away.

"I have something that works much better than a ladle," Grey Cloak suggested.

Nelly turned toward him and said, "What is that?"

"Open your big mouth, and I'll show you."

Nelly's jaw dropped, and she said, "How dare—"

Grey Cloak doused her from head to toe in the bucket of water, and Nelly let out a bloodcurdling shriek. He ran like the devil.

14

GREY CLOAK DUG INTO THE DIRT AND SLUNG A shovelful over his shoulder. He was standing shoulder deep in a pit that he'd been digging all day long.

Rhonna was sitting on a log on the rim of the pit, smoking her pipe. It was early evening, and the sun had settled on the horizon. "You came to me a few years ago, begging for something to eat. I fed you. You wanted shelter. I gave it to you. And this is how you repay me? By insulting the king of Portham's cousins."

Grey Cloak bridled his tongue. He'd made his case to no avail. It only drew Rhonna's ire. He could hear Dyphestive grunting and digging in another pit beside his. His brawny blood brother knew when to keep silent.

Rhonna puffed on her pipe and said, "I will tell you

something. I saved you a great deal of misery. Do you want to know why?"

He flung dirt out of the pit.

"I will tell you why," she continued. "Reputation. That knight is an acquaintance of mine. If not for him, you would be taken to Portham, locked in a stockade, and made an example of. If you think that your back burns now, you should try that."

Grey Cloak stuck his shovel in the dirt, pushed his foot down on the head, and scooped a hunk of clay out. *I really don't care what you have to say because I am leaving. Prattle on all that you want, dwarf. I'm not listening.*

"Royalty has a frivolous manner of dispensing justice. Often, it can be extreme. Why, you might have swung from the gallows or lost your head to a guillotine. Perhaps they would have snipped off your tongue." She made a raspy chuckle. "Even I've thought of that.

"Striplings. When you are young, you think you are invincible. Instead, you are headstrong and stupid." She huffed out rings of smoke. "Brashness can get you killed." She leaned over the pit. "It's nice hearing the evening wind instead of your whining voice."

He forced a tight smile.

"In a few more seasons, you'll be men. That's when the real chores begin." She started humming a sad-sounding tune.

The song droned on for another hour, then finally, she

stood up, shook the tobacco from her pipe, and said, "That will do. Put the shovels up. I'll see you both in the morning."

After Rhonna walked off, he let out a sigh. "Thank goodness." He threw his shovel topside and climbed out then looked down at Dyphestive. His hole was twice as deep. "Well done. You've dug yourself a hole that you can't get out of."

"Can too." Dyphestive tossed his shovel up to Grey Cloak. He jumped, hooked his fingers on the rim, and pulled himself out. "Told you. That was easy."

"Yes, very impressive. Come along now. I'm ready for a nice, cozy sleep among the pigs and chickens."

"Me too."

"I was being sarcastic."

"I know."

Grey Cloak took the shovels into the forge and leaned them in their spots against the wall. The coals in the furnace still glowed orange, and he stretched his fingers over the warmth. "My beautiful hands are going to look like jerky before all of this is said and done." He rubbed his palms. "Aren't you tired of it?"

"I don't mind it."

"What about that spoiled princess, Nelly? What kind of name is that? Did her toothy parents name her after a horse?"

Dyphestive chuckled. "You think about things too much."

"No, I don't. I don't think about them enough." He began pacing. "I feel the need for something greater, feel a yearning inside of me. I see no reason why I can't have a castle of my own one day. Or be a baron of fields of farmland. I want something more."

"The happiest man is the man that wishes to be no happier."

"You listen to Rhonna too much."

"I heard a woman sing it in the village." Dyphestive leaned against the huge anvil, crossed his meaty arms over his chest, and yawned. "Let's get some rest."

"It's too early to go to bed, and I don't sleep much, anyway." Something caught his eye. He stared at the anvil. It had been scooted a half inch from its petrified base. "Move away."

"Huh?"

"Step away from the anvil."

Dyphestive gave him a funny look but complied. He looked down at the anvil.

Grey Cloak traced his finger along the bottom edge. A lighter outline went around the rim. "It's been moved."

"It gets hit all of the time. Of course it moved."

"No, not this anvil. It never moves. Not unless someone moved it." His fingers dusted the top of the anvil. "Do you remember what Rhonna said? She said we'll be men when we can move the anvil."

"She's only jesting. That's dead weight. We can't lift it."

"You can. I know you can. You're big enough now."

Dyphestive shook his head.

"I know you tried before, but that was years ago. You *can* do it now. I believe in you."

"What do you want me to lift it for?"

"Call it a hunch."

With a grunt, Dyphestive wrapped his powerful arms around the anvil.

"Lift with your back and your legs."

"I know." Dyphestive tightened his lock, squeezed the anvil, and tried to lift it. "Hurk!" The veins in his neck started to rise, and the anvil inched off of the platform.

"You're doing it. Lift it higher."

"How much higher?" Dyphestive asked through clenched teeth.

Grey Cloak showed the span between his thumb and index finger. "Just this much."

Dyphestive inched the anvil higher up his body. "I can't hold it much longer," he groaned. "It's heavier than it looks!"

A black hole was below the anvil. "I knew it," Grey Cloak said. He snaked his hand into the hole."

"It's coming down," Dyphestive warned. "It's slipping through my sweating fingers!"

"A moment longer." He had half of his forearm in the hole.

Dyphestive dropped the anvil.

15

"Oy! You almost got me," Grey Cloak said as he jerked his hand away. He waggled his dagger. "I found it."

Dyphestive thumbed the sweat from his eyes. "Good for you. Now what are you going to do with it?"

Tucking the dagger in his belt, Grey Cloak said, "I'm going to fetch my cloak and head to Raven Cliff."

"Don't do that. Rhonna will come after us."

"She will not. Shepherds and farmhands quit all the time. And who can blame them? Who could blame us? It's time to venture out and find our own fortune. See the world. Seek treasure."

"But the Doom Riders. Won't they still be searching for us?"

"They wouldn't know our faces if they saw them. Both

of us have sprouted, and look at you—you have whiskers growing on your face."

Dyphestive scratched his head and sighed. "We don't have any coin, and I don't have a weapon."

Grey Cloak pointed at the wall. "There are plenty over there."

"I'm not stealing. Not from Rhonna."

"Don't worry. I have my dagger and wits, and you have your brawn. We'll be fine. We made it all the way down here on our own. A jaunt to Raven Cliff will be a breeze."

Dyphestive nodded. "All right. But only because you are my brother and Rhonna is not my mother."

"Thankfully." Grey Cloak peered outside and saw no sign of Rhonna. She had a stone house that was little more than a shed. Once she went in for the night, she didn't come out. "Come on, before anyone notices and asks any questions."

Dyphestive grabbed a small anvil that was abandoned in the junk pile of the smithy.

"What is that for?" Grey Cloak asked.

"A keepsake," Dyphestive said as he put the anvil in a potato sack and tucked it under his arm like a pet.

"Brother, you have issues." Grey Cloak headed outside to the barn and grabbed his cloak. He led the way down the road, moving east at a brisk pace.

Dyphestive's arms swung at his sides. At the top of a

rise in the road, he took one long last look back and said, "Goodbye, Rhonna. Thank you."

"Yes, goodbye, you ol' back breaker." Grey Cloak gave his brother a shove in the back. "It's time, brother. Are you sure you want to go?"

"I go wherever you go."

"I'm glad to hear it. Now stop frowning. A new life lies just over the horizon. Let's run for it."

They started to run just as storm clouds rumbled and lightning streaked through the sky.

"THEY'RE GONE," Rhonna said to Griff.

She was standing inside the forge, looking at the anvil, which was askew. Griff was a burly part-orc, part-ogre, part-ugly farmhand. He was a towering seven feet tall and had long arms that hung to his knees. Griff worked the forge on the southern side of Havenstock almost a league away.

She eyed the anvil and said, "See if you can lift that."

Griff lumbered over to the anvil. His black fingernails were like metal files. He locked his hands around the anvil, grunted, and lifted it. His body shook, and the corded muscles underneath his hairy forearms twitched.

Rhonna reached in the hole. "The dagger's gone. I'll be." She pulled her hand back. "I'm done."

Griff dropped the anvil into place with a huff. His lone

remaining ear wiggled. "Do you think the stripling lifted this?"

"He's the only one that could have. I knew there was something different about that boy and the elf the day I met them." She grabbed her apron off the rack and dropped it over her shoulders then tied it behind her back. "Gone is gone. Nothing I can do about it now."

Griff scratched the remaining patch of hair on his head. His face was all scars and pits. "Do you think they are—"

"Don't utter it. We can't afford to let those words be taken in the wind. Only trouble can come from it." She walked over to the furnace and started pumping the bellows, and the coals began to glow bright orange. "We don't want to make that sort of assumption. Let's go about our business like we've been doing." She leaned back and cracked her back. "It's been such a long time since I tasted the sting of battle. It's not our problem now."

Griff walked to a back corner of the room. Some old weapons stood upright there. Among them was a corroded two-handed sword covered in dust and remnants of cobwebs. He pulled it free of the cluster of weapons. With his long fingers, he gently brushed the dust and grit from the scabbard.

"What do you think you are doing?" She stopped pumping the bellows. "Put that back."

"The moment I fit the pommel in my hand, something runs through me. My blood begins to churn." His smile revealed many broken teeth. "I know you miss it, Rhonna. I see the fire in your eyes. Your tireless work. You beat that anvil like a war drum."

Thunder clapped, lightning lit up the sky, and a downpour began.

"Put it back, Griff. Those days are over."

Griff placed the sword back in the corner and said, "A soldier's war is never over. Not for the likes of us."

16

Dyphestive's tummy rumbled. It had been groaning nonstop for miles. "We need to get something to eat."

"We will," Grey Cloak assured him. "I don't see what your problem is. We ate only a day ago."

Holding his belly, Dyphestive said, "Those were raw potatoes, and they only go so far. They don't taste very good, either. We should have hunted. I could have at least snared a fox or a rabbit."

"What were you going to do? Kill them with your anvil? You hate killing animals."

"No, I don't. Well, I like eating them but not so much killing them. I was going to let you do that."

Grey Cloak wrung the rain out of the corner of his cloak. The skies were clear again. "I'm not going to waste any time chasing rabbits. We'll be fine once we get to Raven Cliff. There will be food aplenty. Besides, you won't die from starvation, and it wouldn't kill you to miss a meal now and again."

They had walked and run nonstop through the day and part of the night, fighting through sheets of torrential rains and climbing the muddy hills. With determination, they trekked on, avoiding any people they saw before they were spotted.

Grey Cloak took off at a sprint and didn't stop until he was on top of a rise of wildflowers. He waved his arm in a full circular motion. "There it is! There it is!"

Dyphestive jogged up to him.

Grey Cloak pointed. "That must be Raven Cliff."

Dyphestive rolled his hand underneath his nose. "That must be food cooking." A smile broadened on his face. "Yes! It's coming from the city." He took off running.

Raven Cliff was perched on a league-long stretch of cliffs that rose only fifty feet over the fields and smaller villages. Much like Havenstock, the valley was rich in farmland, but the buildings on the cliffs were different. The city itself was a network of wooden buildings with high-pitched clay-shingled roofs.

Grey Cloak quickly caught up with Dyphestive, and they took one of the cobblestone roads that led up a steep bend toward the city. They passed people of all varieties, ranging from elves and dwarves to orcs, halflings, and men.

The people were lively and direct and moved with purpose. Soldiers in chain mail rode on horseback, keeping a watchful eye on the citizens.

They crested the hill.

"Whoa," Dyphestive said.

Even Grey Cloak couldn't believe his eyes. The sprawling city went on and on, block after block, with no end in sight. Horses and wagons clattered over the streets, which twisted in gentle S shapes.

A soldier on horseback approached them. He was wearing chain mail underneath a leather tunic and carried a sword in his hip scabbard. The well-armed man said, "What business do you have here?"

"Er..." Grey Cloak straightened his back and said, "We are picking up a package of linens for Havenstock. Could you direct us to the seamstress guild?"

"The guilds are in the north quadrant of the city. Guild Row, we call it." The hard-eyed soldier leaned toward them and spoke in a dangerous voice. "We don't tolerate disorder of any kind in this city. If we catch a thief, we hang them. You'll see the gallows on your way down."

Grey Cloak saluted. "Yes, Sergeant. We fully understand. We'll be on our way." He grabbed his brother's arm and pulled him off the street. "Right away."

"That wasn't a very friendly greeting," Dyphestive said.

"We don't exactly look like two people that are in good order." He noticed urchins running through the streets, begging for money, and dashing into the alleys. "We look more like beggars than farmhands. It's time to do something about that."

They'd been to Havenstock plenty of times over the years. Though Havenstock was smaller and simpler in layout than Raven Cliff, they were still pretty much the same. With hustle in their steps, they headed north to where the majority of the guildhalls and marketplaces were located.

"Do you even know where we are going?" Dyphestive asked. "I want to get something to eat." He sniffed loudly. "I can smell food everywhere. And garbage. I think I could eat that too."

"You'll be fed soon enough. You didn't have to come, you know. You're slowing me down," he said as they hurried down the covered porch.

A heavyset man in a worn leather tunic teetered out of the swinging doors of a tavern. He bumped into Dyphestive, stumbled, and fell down the short flight of two steps.

Dyphestive walked toward the man and reached down to try to help him up.

The man pulled a dagger and slashed at his ankles. "I'll kill you!" he slurred. "Push me down, will you. No one —hiccup—shoves Arn Andy and lives to tell—hic—about it."

"I was only trying to help. You are the one that bumped into me," Dyphestive fired back.

"You pushed me!" Arn scrambled to his feet and slashed wildly.

Grey Cloak seized his brother by the wrist and said, "Ignore him. Keep going. He'll forget about it. He's as drunk as an orcen sailor."

Dyphestive backed away from the man.

Arn gave him a wild-eyed look. "You coward!" he slurred. "What's the matter? You afraid to fight an old man?"

"I'm no coward, and if you weren't drunk, I would throttle you," Dyphestive replied.

A group of husky men in leather tunics exited the same tavern the chubby man had stumbled out of. All of them had short hair in the front and long hair in the back. Their beards were bushy, and each was carrying a flagon of wine.

The shortest member waddled to the end of the porch and leaned against a post. He took a drink from his flagon and in a deep voice asked, "What seems to be the problem, Father?"

Arn pointed at Dyphestive, hiccupped, and said, "These two rapscallions tried to rob me, Tiny!"

"Is that right?" Tiny glowered at the blood brothers. He shattered his flagon on the porch. "Well, that makes me mad. Brothers, kill them!"

17

THE GROUP OF SLUGGARDS MOVED IN SLOW MOTION BY Grey Cloak's standards. He could have been a few blocks away before they hopped off the porch, and he could have disappeared into the alleys. But the same couldn't be said for Dyphestive. He was standing in the street like a bull waiting for the charge. The motley crew of men jumped on top of him, and they went down to the ground in a tangle of flailing limbs.

A thug with silver hoop earrings zeroed in on Grey Cloak. He reached out and swiped at him. "Stand still, elf. I want to cut those pointy ears off and make a necklace out of them."

"That sounds disgusting." Grey Cloak kicked the thug's legs from underneath him, and the man's head hit the cobblestones with a *crack*. He stepped on the man's big belly and sprang into the knot of his brother's attackers. Fastening his arms around the thug father's neck, he said, "You shouldn't have started trouble with us, fool!"

The father of the thugs clawed at Grey Cloak's arms. He coughed and spat and croaked out, "Get off me!"

"Call your boys off," he demanded.

"Nooo!" Arn waddled backward and drove Grey Cloak back first into a porch post. Then he kept ramming him into the post. *Wham! Wham! Wham!*

Grey Cloak's body shook, and his grip loosened. *This is not how I envisioned it.* Before Arn could ram him into the post again, Grey Cloak slid off the man's back. Arn hit the post so hard that his head snapped back against the post. Grey Cloak grabbed ahold of the man's boot and twisted the foot hard.

"Eeyooow!" Arn cried. He turned around and dropped to his knees, shaking.

Without thinking, Grey Cloak filled his hands with the man's head of hair and rammed his head into the post. "Don't mess with my brother!" *Whomp!* "Or me, for that matter!" *Crack!*

Arn's husky body sagged onto the steps, and his sons began to yell.

"OOF!"

"Ow!"

"Holy cow bladders, what is this boy made of?"

From underneath the pile of thugs, Dyphestive began to emerge. His big arms flailed about his body like an angry windmill. A grim snarl was set on his face. He landed an uppercut in a thug's belly that lifted the man off of his feet. "Get off me!" he roared.

A thug with more beard than hair on his head punched Dyphestive in the jaw. He winced as he shook his hand and said, "He's made of iron. Like a rock!" Then he turned around and started to run.

One. Two. Three. Four. Five. Grey Cloak counted the number of thugs attacking his brother. *Five on foot and two down. And I thought seven was the number of fortune.*

"What are you smirking at, elf?" Tiny asked. He slipped away from Dyphestive's wrath and advanced on Grey Cloak. "You won't be smiling after I stick you like a pig."

"Speaking of pigs, you don't really think that you'll get within a foot of me, do you?" Grey Cloak moved away from the rotund man, keeping his eyes fixed on him the entire time. "You'll only wind yourself."

"I'll slice the wind out of you!" Tiny lunged at Grey Cloak.

He skipped away from the tip of the dagger, casually spun around, and kicked Tiny in the backside. Tiny stumbled forward and crashed into the steps on the porch.

A rugged crowd had spilled out of the tavern and gathered on the porch. They were laughing, and some of them started to applaud.

Grey Cloak made a winning smile and took a bow.

"He hurt Father! Get him!" another brother said. The burly man with a missing ear stormed after Grey Cloak like a charging bull.

Three down, only four to go. Grey Cloak leapt over the charging man, using his shoulder as a step to propel him forward. He did a somersault in the air and landed on the shoulders of one of Dyphestive's attackers.

Dyphestive stood tall in the street. He was winding up his potato sack that had an anvil inside it.

"How are you doing, brother?" Grey Cloak asked.

Dyphestive punched an attacker in the face. "You're going to get us in trouble."

"Get off me!" the thug shouted at Grey Cloak. The man's dirty fingers grabbed at him.

"Would this help?" Grey Cloak covered the man's eyes with his hands.

Dyphestive walloped the man in the gut with the small anvil.

"Oof!" The thug dropped to his knees, clutching his belly.

Grey Cloak hopped off the man's back, dusted off his hands, and said, "Five down and only two to go."

He stood back to back with his brother, and they faced the last two attackers. Dyphestive spun his unique weapon like windmill blades in a thunderstorm. The thugs balled up their fists and faced them.

"I like these odds. Two against two, and we don't even have a scratch on us," Grey Cloak said. He pulled his dagger. "As for the rest of your brood, well, as you can see"—he glanced at the fallen men—"you can't say the same."

The thugs gathered up the members of their clan. With Arn, the father, and Tiny, the rotten son, in tow, the hobbled thugs fled into the alleys.

"That was well done," Grey Cloak said. He put his dagger away and waved at the onlookers. "The show is over. But we are accepting contribu—"

"Halt! Halt!" A soldier was running down the street toward them. He was accompanied by three other well-armed men.

Grey Cloak took Dyphestive by the wrist and said, "Run!"

18

"I THINK THE WAY IS CLEAR," GREY CLOAK SAID. HE crawled out of a haystack in a large stable. The horses in the stalls nickered and snorted. He stood up, crept to the stable entrance, and looked both ways down the road. No soldiers were in the streets. "Come on, Dyphestive." He looked back at the pile of hay he'd hidden inside. "Dyphestive?"

The pile of hay was snoring. He hurried over and cleared away the hay, uncovering Dyphestive's big face. His blood brother was sleeping with a content look on his face.

"What are you dreaming about now? I bet you're eating something." He pinched his brother on the cheek.

Dyphestive's eyelids popped open, and he fixed his gaze on his brother. "Did you pinch me?"

"Yes."

"Why would you do that? I was having a good dream. I

was with the Sky Rider. What was her name? Anya?" He smiled. "Yes, Anya. She kissed me on the cheek." He rubbed his face. "And that was when you woke me."

"Yes, so sorry about that. Now get up. We need to find a trading post and get some money." Grey Cloak's tummy rumbled, and he put his hand on his belly. "After all that running, I'm a tad hungry myself."

Dyphestive stood up. He looked like a living haystack and began dusting himself off and picked many strands of straw out of his hair. "What about the soldiers? Won't they be looking for us?"

Grey Cloak looked outside again. A heavy rain had started coming down. "It seems the clear skies are gone. No one will be looking for us in this rain." He wrapped his cloak around his body. "Come on. Let's find Guild Row."

They made their way north, keeping to the alleys and plodding through the sloppy road. Dyphestive stomped through every puddle they passed.

"Will you quit doing that?"

"Doing what? This?" Dyphestive leapt upward and forward and brought both feet down in a huge ankle-deep puddle. The water splashed all over Grey Cloak. "Hah!"

"I'm already wet."

"Now you are wetter." Dyphestive stepped out of the puddle. "We really need to eat soon."

They emerged from the alley and entered Guild Row. All sorts of buildings and shops were in a long row down the street. Blacksmiths, stonecutters, woodworkers, jewelers, fragrance crafters, alchemists, seamstresses, and all sorts were busy manufacturing goods inside their stores. Wagons with teams of horses were loaded and sent on their way. Halflings carrying wooden boxes on their shoulders hustled through the streets.

"I smell food," Dyphestive said. His nose crinkled, and he headed for a row of pies sitting on a windowsill underneath a porch roof. "I could eat all of those."

"Be patient." Grey Cloak spied an odd building at the northeast quadrant of Guild Row. Crammed between two run-down taverns but standing taller than both of them, it was an ugly building made of grayed wood paneling that wasn't in good order. A wooden sign that swung on links of chain hung over the porch front. The sign read in faded white lettering: Batram's Bartery and Arcania. White lightning bolts on both ends of the lettering twinkled like stars. "There, a barter shop. We can make a good deal here."

Dyphestive looked the shabby building up and down. "I hope it doesn't fall on top of us." He followed Grey Cloak up the steps, and the floorboards groaned loudly. "Zooks. I don't even think the porch will hold."

They stood on the porch, staring at the dull black door with paint peeling off of it that led into the building, which wasn't very wide compared to the buildings beside it. It looked more like it had been used to fill in an alley. They exchanged a look.

Scratching his head, Dyphestive said, "Are you sure you want to go in there? It doesn't look like a typical trading post."

"This isn't a farm town like Havenstock. This is a real city, complete with everything. Don't worry. I'll do the talking. You keep quiet and don't touch anything." Grey Cloak reached for the door handle, but there wasn't one. "That's odd. Hmm, I guess we have to knock." He made a fist and raised it to strike, but the black door swung open.

Someone with a deep, resonant voice called to them from within. "Come in."

Grey Cloak stepped forward at the same time that Dyphestive did, and they were momentarily jammed shoulder to shoulder in the doorway.

Popping through, Grey Cloak said, "Stay behind me."

Dyphestive nodded and fell in place. The moment they crossed the threshold, the door shut behind them. A brisk wind picked up, blowing their clothing like a windstorm, and they shed water like dogs. Then the wind stopped as suddenly as it started. Grey Cloak patted himself down, and he was as dry as a bone. He looked around, and the inside of the building was very dim.

"Wipe your feet," the deep-voiced person said.

"Certainly." Grey Cloak looked down at his bare feet. He was standing on a rug made from a huge razorback hog.

It had a head bigger than two men, and its pitch-black

eyes moved when it spoke. "Hurry up! Wipe and get off me."

He and Dyphestive started wiping their feet.

"Oh, that's the spot," the razorback rug said. "Dig in. I like that. Please, take your time."

"This is weird," Dyphestive said. "I think we should leave."

The store foyer fell into complete darkness. "No one is going anywhere."

19

"Stop rustling about! You are in my shop, and you will live, or I would not have let you in. I treat all of my customers well. The cooperative ones, that is."

Dyphestive breathed heavily, and Grey Cloak's heart thumped quickly. Flames came to life and danced on the wicks of many candles, and slowly, a warm light spread throughout the store. They were standing in front of a large counter made from black mahogany and shielded with panes of glass. It came up to Grey Cloak's chin. Behind the counter were walls of shelving and black drawers. The shelving was the same black wood, and each drawer had a corroded brass handle. The larger drawers were on the bottom, and the smaller ones were on top. The shelves displayed a variety of jewelry, hand-crafted weapons, gold and silver flatware, and gifts. It all appeared to be worth a fortune.

Grey Cloak poked the glass with a finger. "Look at that." He pointed at a gravy boat made of solid gold. "Who would spend a fortune on such a thing?"

Dyphestive shrugged. "I wonder if it makes gravy taste any better."

"Don't touch the glass! You'll smudge it."

Grey Cloak looked about but didn't see the source of the spunky voice. He wiped the glass with his cloak. "Sorry, er, Batram?"

"Very good. The shoeless elf can read a sign. I'm very busy. What do you want?"

Grey Cloak looked at Dyphestive, and Dyphestive shrugged at him. He couldn't help but think of how easy it would be to steal something from the counter case and run away. He looked over his shoulder and saw that the black door was gone. So was the razorback rug.

"Heh-heh-heh. You think to run away, do you? Steal from my shop. I know it is tempting. I suggest that you perish the thought. None may enter, and none may go unless I say so."

"Are we being held captive?" Grey Cloak asked.

"Of course not. You may go whenever you wish. But I am curious about why you came."

Dyphestive rose on tiptoe and leaned over the counter. Under his breath he said, "I don't see anyone. Do you?"

"No," Grey Cloak replied. "Not yet." He cleared his throat. "I wanted to trade something."

"*You?* I mean no offense, but you don't appear to have anything to offer." A hollow chuckle carried throughout the store. "You don't even own a good pair of shoes."

"I have good boots," Dyphestive commented.

"I'm faster without shoes," Grey Cloak added. "And better off without them. Perhaps we should take our business elsewhere."

"Tsk, tsk, tsk," Batram said. "Don't be so thin-skinned, stripling. I am only getting to know you. I pride myself on a strong personal relationship with my customers."

Grey Cloak didn't see any sign of anyone talking. His eyes slid over the walls and shelves. The only things moving were the spiders in the cobwebs. "Are you invisible?"

"Of course not. Invisibility is a great power. A wondrous power." Batram cleared his throat. "And I am not a ghost, either. I'm certain that you would have asked that next, but I am not. This isn't about you seeing me. This is about me seeing you and what you have to offer. If you carry something of value, I want to see what it is. Put it on the counter."

Grey Cloak reached into his belt, pulled out the dagger, and set it on the counter.

"A knife? I have many knives," Batram said.

"No, a dagger. It was made with the finest craftsmanship, the likes of which I have never seen. And I've worked in a forge most of my life." He reached for the dagger. "But if you aren't interested..."

"Stop! I didn't say I wasn't interested. I only said that I have many knives. And I wanted to see if you knew the difference. Many can't tell one blade from the other. They wouldn't know a butter knife from a short sword. I've seen all sorts." Batram sighed. "I can see the quality is excellent. What do you want for it?"

Dyphestive's stomach let out a wild growl.

"Ah, I bet that you want something to eat, don't you?" Batram said. "Tell me... where did you steal this dagger from?"

"We didn't steal it," Grey Cloak said. "And I don't see how that is of concern to you."

"You don't? Why, it's a great concern of mine. You see, the story behind the dagger can enhance the value."

Grey Cloak's brow furrowed. *He's snowing us.*

"I see you are confused, but let me explain," Batram said. "Take a look inside my display case. On the bottom shelf, you will see a dagger not so different from yours. It is high quality, right?"

He squatted down and looked at the dagger in the case. It rested beside its scabbard, which was lacquered in blood red and had tiny rubies in it. The handle of the dagger matched the scabbard. The double-edged blade caught the candlelight. "It's impressive."

"To many, it might appear to be a ceremonial dagger,

something that the monarchs hand out to their guests as gifts. But," Batram said with a growing excitement, "that dagger was used to kill a dragon. And not just any dragon, but the dragon of Sulter Slay."

20

"I've never heard of it, and I don't see why that matters," Grey Cloak responded.

"Of course not. You are young and foolish," Batram said. "But to many, the story is more valuable than the item."

"I couldn't care less," he fired back.

Dyphestive said, "I want to hear the story about the dragon."

"No, you don't. And how do you know that he's not making the story up to sell his goods?"

The store shook, the drawers rattled, and the candles' light flickered. Batram's resonant voice became thunder. "I am not a liar! I am not some wretched merchant from the Morlan! I am Batram. My word is as good as gold! Do you want to do business with me or not?"

"I do," Dyphestive said. He was holding his belly. "I'm starving."

"It would help if I could see who I was talking to," Grey Cloak said.

"You are an impudent youth." Batram sniffed, and his voice softened when he said, "So be it."

At the tip-top of the shelving, something stirred. An insect-like creature as big as a medium-sized dog began descending the drawers. It looked like a giant tarantula with six long, hairy legs and had the face of a man.

Grey Cloak's heart jumped into his throat. He elbowed Dyphestive and pointed upward. Dyphestive looked up and gulped.

The spider-creature cast a web from its behind. Attached to the webbing line, it swung from one side of the shelving to the other, then it stopped on the drawers ten yards above their heads. It had an impish face of a halfling. Its ears were pointed but slightly rounded, and a curly beard covered its face. "Don't look so alarmed," Batram said. "I don't bite." He jumped onto the counter.

Grey Cloak and Dyphestive jumped backward.

Batram chuckled. "I love doing that to new clients." He was no longer in the body of a spider, but instead, he was standing on two legs and looked like a six-armed halfling. His gray-and-white-striped suit fit him like a glove. He picked up the dagger and tossed it high in the air. "Let's get a better feel for this, shall we."

End over end, the dagger spun through the air. It seemed to pause at its zenith for a moment then plummeted back toward the counter and landed right between Batram's feet. He bent over and plucked the dagger from the counter. He only had two arms and two legs now, and his clothing fit him perfectly.

Grey Cloak blinked. The halfling had changed three times in the wink of a lash.

"Perfectly balanced." Batram thumbed the edge and held it to his ear. "It sings to me. Yes, this is a well-crafted dagger. The metal is mended with magic. Where did you say that you got it?"

"I didn't."

Batram paced across his counter. The halfling stood little more than three feet tall. He tossed the dagger from hand to hand with the skill of a natural juggler. "A street-wise stripling. What a surprise. Listen, if you stole it, well, you stole it. The only issue with me is who you stole it from." He stopped and faced Grey Cloak. "Did you pilfer it from a monarch?"

"No."

"Good. I don't need their kind rattling my cage." Batram extended his hand. His hands were small, but he had long fingers. "As you have deciphered, I am Batram, owner of the arcania. And you are?"

"Do we have to give our names?" Grey Cloak asked but didn't offer his hand.

Batram tugged at the cotton hairs on his chin and said, "No, it's only a courtesy."

"I'm Dyphestive," he said, extending his hand. His hand swallowed Batram's.

"My, you have huge hands for a youth. Strong too." Batram winced and pulled his grip away. "Nice to meet you, er, Dyphestive." His eyes slid over to Grey Cloak, and he offered his hand. "And you are?"

"Grey Cloak," he said, reluctantly shaking Batram's hand.

"You are named after a garment."

"Why does everyone say that?"

"I think the answer to that question is obvious." Batram plopped down on the counter, his short legs dangling over the edge, and he stuck the dagger in the black mahogany. Rubbing his hands together, he said, "Let's do business. What are you wanting for the dagger? Do you want to sell it to me, or do you want to use it for collateral?"

Dyphestive said, "What is collateral?"

"I'm a lender. If you want to borrow money from me, you can use the dagger as *collateral*. I give you some coins, and when you want the dagger back, you can have it back." He patted the counter. "Everything beneath me is collateral. Almost all of it is collateral that is now unclaimed, and I can sell it or trade it."

Grey Cloak rubbed his finger underneath his nose. "How much collateral is the dagger worth?"

"Hmm, I'd give you twenty silver chips."

"That's *all*? I would expect nothing less than one hundred."

"If I knew you better, I would offer fifty chips, but I don't. However, I will buy it from you for the fifty silver."

"For a magic dagger? It must be worth ten times that. Perhaps fifty." Grey Cloak's face reddened. "I'll take my business to the street." He reached for the dagger.

Batram smacked his hand away. "Don't reach over my counter. We are negotiating. Listen to me—I am offering you a fair deal. Twenty silver is more than enough to fill your bellies and take care of yourselves. And you are able. You can earn twenty silver in a week in this town between the two of you. Can't you?"

"I'm really hungry, Grey," Dyphestive said.

"Yes, well, so am I." He looked Batram dead in the eyes. "Make it thirty."

"Twenty-five."

"Deal."

Batram passed his hand over the dagger, and it vanished. Two stacks of silver coins appeared. "Nice doing business with you."

Grey Cloak swiped the coins off the table and said, "I should have asked for forty."

"It wouldn't have changed a thing." Batram pointed at the storefront. "There is the door, striplings. Until we meet again, your dagger will be waiting."

"Nice to meet you," Dyphestive said.

The black door had returned, and so had the razorback rug, but that time, it didn't speak.

Grey Cloak and Dyphestive cast one last look back over their shoulders. A monstrous man over ten feet tall was standing behind the black counter, wearing a tattered gray-and-white suit with the sleeves missing. He had a head like a spider, eight sets of ruby-red eyes, and massive arms layered in muscle. He waved one of his spider legs while the others loaded goods into the drawers. With a flip of his wrist, he shooed them away.

Not daring to look back again, they hustled out the door and into the rain. The black door to Batram's Bartery and Arcania slammed shut behind them.

21

GREY CLOAK SCOFFED AT HIS BROTHER AND SAID, "Nice to meet you."

Dyphestive was sitting with his nose practically in his plateful of hot food. He stuffed two biscuits in his mouth at once then looked up. "Huh?"

"Nothing." Grey Cloak turned his attention to the tavern they were in. It was a lively place filled with people who had come in from the rain. Two fireplaces were burning brightly with orange fire. Barmaids hustled between the tables with trays of food. The smell of greasy meat and baked bread wafted heavily through the air. As he watched so many others eat heartily, he pushed his plate away.

With his mouth full of food, Dyphestive asked, "Aren't you going to eat that?"

"I've had enough. Help yourself."

Dyphestive's eyes widened, and he took his brother's plate and scraped the food on top of his. "You don't have to tell me twice."

Grey Cloak sipped on a cup of hot coffee served in a ceramic mug then poured cream into it and drank more of the bitter drink. Someone bumped into his back, and the coffee sloshed over the rim and started to spill over, but he caught it back inside his cup.

Dyphestive huffed a laugh. "You're fast."

"Yes, I'm even faster than your ability to digest food."

"What are you sore about? We have the chips. The food is good, and we can buy somewhere to sleep." He licked the biscuit butter from his fingers. "I couldn't be happier."

Grey Cloak put his elbows on the table and leaned forward. "Do you have any idea what happened? I've been taken. We've been taken. It's embarrassing."

"You didn't have to take the deal."

"No, I didn't, but I did for your sake. If you didn't have to eat every hour, I might have had time to make a better deal."

"Don't blame me, but if it's all the same, I'm grateful."

Grey Cloak looked at the silver chips in the palm of his hand. It seemed like a paltry sum to receive in exchange for an enchanted dagger. "I wonder how much it was really worth," he muttered.

Dyphestive patted his stomach and let out a very long

and loud belch. The surrounding crowd stopped in their tracks.

"Embarrassing." Grey Cloak pinched his nose.

Some of the patrons chuckled, and a hardy man patted Dyphestive on the back.

Another laborer said, "That's the sort of sound my wife likes to hear. You should come up with me for dinner. She would love that."

Dyphestive shook hands with the strong-armed man and said, "Thanks." He nodded. "I like Raven Cliff. Good food. Good people."

"Don't plan on settling. We have to stay on the move, but I don't think it would kill us to stay here awhile. At least long enough to settle our debt with Batram." Grey Cloak drummed his finger on the table. "And track down that little thief, Zora."

"Zora?" Dyphestive sawed through a hunk of roasted ham. "You don't honestly think that you are going to find her here, do you? She could be anywhere else but here. She was lying to you."

"As if you would know. No, I think that she is here. At least, she stopped here. If I were an elf with a sick grand-mother, where would I be?" He hooked his arm over the back of his chair and noticed a small group of pretty girls—elf and human—looking at him. He raised an eyebrow, smiled, and fluttered his fingers at them.

The girls huddled over their table, giggling loudly. One

of them was looking at his dirty bare feet. She mumbled something, and they started laughing harder.

He crossed his feet, trying to hide one under the other, and turned his back so that his feet couldn't be seen. "I'm going to find a tailor. It would do you well to be fitted in some new clothing as well."

Dyphestive looked at his wool vest and said, "I like what I have on just fine."

"Says the shepherd. If we are going to stay here, then we need to look like we matter. We'll find better work because of it."

"I'll be fine."

"No, you won't." He slid one of the silver pieces across the table. "When you finish eating, go to the room. Have a hireling draw a bath and wash your clothing. I'll meet you in the room later."

"Where are you going?"

"This elf needs new clothes." Grey Cloak stood and started to leave. He stole a glance at the girls, who were still looking at him and laughing. He drew his ragged cloak tighter over his shoulders and headed outside and onto the porch.

The rain had died down, and people were milling through the streets again. Determined not to ask for directions, he plodded along, taking in every building in sight. He prided himself on having knowledge of all things. Every alley was an escape route. The taverns and shops had back doors that he could escape through. The rooftops were slanted and shingled in most cases, but not all. He envisioned himself racing over the rooftops on feet as light as feathers, bounding over the dormers, swinging by the chimneys, and leaving his pursuers behind. *No one can catch me.*

After he covered a few blocks, he came upon a tailor and cobbler shop, so he bounced up the porch steps and entered through the open doors. It had racks of clothing and bins full of shirts and trousers. Rows of shoes and boots were in the back, and he headed that way. He bent down and picked up a pair of soft leather boots with low tops and laces.

A soft tap landed on his shoulder, and someone said in a sweet voice, "May I help you?"

He turned, and his gaze fixed on a pair of green eyes as warm as a fire. "Zora!"

22

ZORA'S EYES GREW, BUT SHE QUICKLY REGAINED HER composure and said, "I beg your pardon. Have we met before?"

Grey Cloak tossed the boots down, marched her backward, and said, "*Have we met?* Don't you dare try to pretend that we haven't. How is your grandmother, Zora? Huh?" He got nose to nose with her. "Where are my spoils?"

Zora the half elf slipped away from him and said, "Young man, I don't know what you are talking about. I've never seen you before in my life. But identities are often mistaken in Raven Cliff. So many from all over come and go."

He clamped his hand around her wrist. There was no mistaking Zora with any other woman. The style of her short auburn hair had not changed, her eyes were as green as spring fields, and her teardrop face was as captivating as ever. "Don't you play games with me. You fooled me once. It won't happen again. Where is my money?"

"Unhand me, farmhand!" she shouted.

Many people were in the store, and they stopped what they were doing and looked dead at them.

A slender man who was nicely dressed in a cotton shirt and trousers and had an apron over the top walked over. His waxen hair was feathery. Politely, he asked, "What seems to be the problem, Zora?"

Her brow momentarily furrowed.

"Ah, so it is Zora!" Grey Cloak exclaimed.

"Don't listen to this vagrant, Tanlin," she argued as she twisted her wrist out of his grip. "He was trying to pilfer a pair of shoes."

"I was not. I came to purchase a pair of boots, among other items," he said.

"Zora, you know my standard. We treat all of our customers the same. Help me with what he needs." Tanlin eyed Grey Cloak up and down. "Assuming you can pay for it."

Grey Cloak showed his small coin purse and shook it. "Plenty." He tucked it away, staring at Zora.

Tanlin rubbed his prominent chin and said to Zora, "Suit the young man up."

Zora frowned. "As you wish." She shoved Grey Cloak.

"Come on. We need to get you in some new clothing. You stink."

"You are the one that stinks. Now give me my money," he demanded.

"I don't have it." She grabbed a folded brick-red shirt and a pair of cotton trousers dyed black and shoved the items against his chest. "Try these on." She pushed him into a dressing room that only showed his feet and head and leaned against it. "If I did, I would give it to you. But I needed it to take care of my sick grandmother."

"Sure, you did." He flipped his shirt over the door, hitting her in the face.

"Ew!" She moved away, grabbed the leather shoes he'd pulled out earlier, and tossed them over the door.

"Ow!"

She giggled. "That didn't hurt."

"No, maybe not, but your robbery of my items did."

"Come now, you stole them from someone else, and I stole them from you."

"Ah, so you admit it!" He stepped out of the dressing room wearing the shirt, the trousers, and the boots. His tattered cloak hung over his shoulders.

"Will you lose this rag?" She took the cloak out of his hand and tossed it onto the floor. Then she gave an approving nod. "That's better. You look very... dapper." Her nose crinkled. "Once you wash the stink off. Hmmm, we sell perfume."

"I'm not wearing perfume."

She rolled her eyes and said, "Why doesn't that surprise me? Everyone adores the smell of shepherd."

"Hah!" He poked his finger at her. "You remember."

"Of course I do, but you aren't going to get your money back. It's gone. Easy come, easy go. You should have been more careful." She pointed at him. "Shall I wrap that up?"

He gave her a dejected look. "You should buy these clothes for me. You owe me."

"I owe you nothing." She fixed the collar on his shirt. "Listen, uh, what was your name again?"

Her soft breath on his face stirred him. He swallowed and said, "Grey Cloak."

"Oh yes, such an original name." She looked him in the eye. "Don't be hurt by this, but you are young, and I hated to take advantage of you, but believe me when I say that I didn't have a choice."

"Believe me, I don't believe you. And you aren't that much older than me, so don't talk to me like I'm some sort of child."

She brushed his hair over his eyes, and he tightened his grip on his purse.

"Do you want to keep your old clothes, or shall I burn them?"

"I'll keep them, thank you."

He walked to the front counter, and she picked up his clothing, folded it up, and followed him. Tanlin was standing behind the counter, dipping a feather in an inkwell.

"How much?"

"Let's see," Tanlin said. "One shirt, one pair of trousers, and a pair of boots. For you, young fella, four silvers."

Grey Cloak slapped the coins on the counter and slid them over.

Zora set the old clothing on the counter. "You really should consider burning this remnant that you call a cloak. It's raggedy. We can fit you in something more suitable."

He gathered up his belongings and said, "I'll manage." With a frown, he walked out of the store, down the steps, and into the street. After he made it one block away, he turned.

Zora was standing in the doorway, watching him with a bewitching smile on her face. She waved at him as he backed away. Her nimble fingers smoothed over the curve of her hips as she patted herself down. A concerned look grew on her face, and her gaze locked on him.

Grey Cloak dangled a pearl-colored silk purse in front of him. He offered her a smile as big as a rainbow, took a bow, laughed, and was quickly on his way.

23

"I WISH YOU COULD HAVE SEEN THE LOOK ON HER FACE, Dyphestive." Grey Cloak was lying on a small bed, tossing Zora's silk purse in the air. "Her cute little chin hit the porch and bounced. I swear it!"

Dyphestive was sitting on the edge of his bed, hanging on his blood brother's every word. "I can't believe you found her. Of all the fortune. We've never had fortune like that." He shifted his position, and the wood-frame bed creaked.

They were inside a small room at the inn they had eaten at earlier. The furnishings were simple. Two small wooden chests were at the ends of the twin beds, a desk had two brass candle stands that were lit, and an octagonal portal window overlooked the city streets. The stuffy room was dim.

"I don't think I can sleep after that. It was so exciting getting her back," Grey Cloak said.

"So what is in the purse?"

"Ah, not all that I'd hoped for." Grey Cloak sat up and crossed his legs and spilled the contents of the pouch into his hands. "A pair of silver hoop earrings, five silver chips, and one gold." He put the treasure back in the purse. "It's not the same haul that she stole from me, but it's enough for me to buy the dagger back, and we won't have to do any backbreaking work, either."

"Don't you think she'll come looking for it?"

"Raven Cliff has so many people that it would be easier to find a needle in a haystack." He lay back on his pillow with his fingers clasped behind his head. "We'll be fine. Besides, it's good to finally get some satisfaction after all the misfortune we've run into. And you thought my efforts were futile."

Dyphestive shrugged. "You have to admit that finding her was dumb luck."

"You say that, but I think it's a matter of my dogged persistence paying off."

Dyphestive rolled his eyes, but Grey Cloak didn't see it. "What are we going to do now that we are here?"

"Seek adventure. In a place like Raven Cliff, there is bound to be some sort of campaign rolling." He rolled over to his side. "Do you remember what that hermit said? The Red Claw tavern that he talked about—we'll go there."

"You're going to follow the guidance of a babbler that tried to keep us jailed when we tried to free him?" Dyphestive flopped back on the bed, making its legs scrape over the floor. "Don't be surprised if you find out that it doesn't exist."

"There's no harm in looking. I'll ask around tomorrow when you are eating breakfast." He tossed the silk purse in the air again and smiled. "Oh, the look on her face."

Knock! Knock! Knock!

They sat up.

"Open up!" someone with a gruff voice said. "We know you are in there!"

Grey Cloak stashed his coin purses under the pillow and looked at his brother, who shrugged. Once he cleared his throat, he said, "Can I help you? We are trying to sleep."

A hard fist pounded on the door. "Don't resist the patrol. Open the door, or we will bust it open."

"You'd better open it," Dyphestive said.

The only thing that came to Grey Cloak's mind was the city patrol that had chased after them earlier in the day. He said quietly, "I'll handle this. Don't you say a word." He opened the door. "Can I help you, Sergeant?" He feigned a yawn and stretched out his arms. "We were sleeping."

"That's him, Constable," a young part-elven woman shrieked. It was Zora. She was standing behind the large man in a constable's uniform. "He's the elf that stole my purse. Him and that big one!"

Three more men stormed down the hallway and flooded the room. They shoved Grey Cloak and Dyphestive down on the floor, shackled their arms behind them, and hauled them to their feet.

Grey Cloak gave Zora an incredulous look as they were shoved out of the door. "How did you find me?"

Zora twisted a strand of her auburn hair around her fingers and said, "Did you really think it would be that difficult? A young elf in black trousers with a very nice brick-red jerkin. Oh, and handsome too." She tugged his chin. "If only you'd worn that rotten gray cloak, it would have been much more difficult to find you."

24

GREY CLOAK AND DYPHESTIVE FOUND THEIR NEW accommodations far less pleasant than the last. They were taken to the dungeon cells at the constable's station. They called it the watchmen's roost. It was one of the places where the soldiers of Raven Cliff gathered for their duties. The cell was made of iron bars and had smelly blankets on the floor. A bucket with a wooden ladle in it sat outside.

Dyphestive had his head buried between his knees. "And I thought I was going to get a good night's sleep."

"At least you are fed," Grey Cloak said. He didn't hide the bitterness in his voice. Zora had gotten him again. *She's made a fool of me twice.* "You'll live."

The watchmen's roost was a small stone building along the main street of the city. It consisted of several holding cells like the one they were in. The floors were a network of stones, and weapons racks of spears, halberds, swords, and crossbows lined the walls. A large wooden desk and a small table sat beside a glass window. Two watchmen in chain mail underneath uniform tunics were playing cards.

Grey Cloak could see his belongings on the large desk. His clothing and his pouch full of silver were on the top.

Two men entered the front door of the roost. One of them was very tall, a ranking sergeant, with a full black beard. The watchmen at the table stood up and saluted. The sergeant jerked his thumb over his shoulder, and the two soldiers hustled out the front door.

The second man was Tanlin, the polished salesman from the tailor shop. He and the sergeant were laughing heartily.

"I hope you enjoyed the meal, Zofar," Tanlin said as he shook the sergeant's hand. "We'll have to make sure we meet again sooner."

"Agreed, Tanlin," Zofar said in a hoarse voice. He eyed Grey Cloak and Dyphestive. "Are you sure you want to bail those two monkeys out?"

"No harm, no foul." Tanlin walked over to the desk and picked up Grey Cloak's bag of coins. "How much for bail?"

"For you, seven chips should do." Zofar stuck his palm out. After Tanlin sprinkled coins into his hand, he closed his hand into a fist. "You know where the key is. Shall I give you some privacy?"

Tanlin nodded and said politely, "That would be appreciated. I won't be long."

Zofar departed, leaving Tanlin, Grey Cloak, and Dyphestive alone in the roost.

Tanlin rolled up the cuffs of his silk shirt to his elbows then picked up a stool, walked it over to the cell, and sat down. He eyed Grey Cloak. "You have very fast fingers. Zora didn't see it, but I did." He clapped softly. "Well done."

"Grey Cloak, who is this?" Dyphestive asked.

"This is the man that ran the store where I found Zora." He kept his eyes on Tanlin. "I see that you pocketed the rest of my chips. Are you here to rob me as well?"

"No, not at all." Tanlin fished the coin purse out of his pocket and tossed it over his shoulder, and it landed back on Grey Cloak's clothing. "I have other intentions."

"Such as?"

"I'm always seeking talent to work at my shop. A stripling with quick fingers could be taught to weave the finest clothing."

Grey Cloak tucked his fingers underneath his arms, leaned back against the bars, and said, "I'm not interested."

Tanlin turned his attention to Dyphestive. "And what about your big friend?"

"Him? I don't think so."

"I can speak for myself," Dyphestive said. He eyed Tanlin. "Not interested."

"I see. So you don't want to earn all of your lost chips back and perhaps acquire more?"

"I didn't lose anything. It was stolen from me," Grey Cloak said. He scooted toward the bars. "What do you mean by 'acquire more'?"

Tanlin made a polite smile and said, "More means more. Gold, silver, gems, among many other items that you could be exposed to. You see, I have a knack for eyeing talent, and I think that the pair of you could be useful."

"You're talking about stealing, aren't you?" Dyphestive said. "I'm not a thief."

"Please, I'm not talking about ordinary pickpockets. Now, this is a different sort of task. It is a campaign into the forbidden."

"Why us?" Grey Cloak asked.

"As I said, I have an eye for talent. Perhaps in your case, it's more of a gut feeling. And Zora is fond of you too. She rather enjoyed your little game." Tanlin smiled.

Turning to Dyphestive, Grey Cloak asked, "What do you think?"

"I want a bed, and I want to sleep."

Grey Cloak returned his attention to the feathery-haired Tanlin and said, "I guess we don't really have a choice, do we. Either we agree, and you let us out, or we don't agree, and we stay."

Tanlin shook his head. "On the contrary, you are free to go." He stuck a key in the lock and twisted it.

Grey Cloak didn't recall seeing the key in his hand before.

"You are free to go," Tanlin said again. He picked up the stool and moved it back over to the desk. "If you are interested, find me at the Red Claw Tavern. Tomorrow night."

Dyphestive and Grey Cloak exchanged a glance.

"That's a real place?" Grey Cloak asked.

Tanlin tilted his head to one side and approached him. "Yes, why? Where have you heard of it before?"

"A hermit told us," he said.

"What sort of hermit?"

"What other kind is there? They live under giant mushrooms or caves. I don't know."

Tanlin's face almost touched the prison cell bars. His creaseless forehead started to crinkle. "Tell me," he said quickly, "what else did this hermit say?"

Grey Cloak shrugged, but Dyphestive added, "Save a dragon. Save the world."

Tanlin looked like he was about to burst, but he quickly regained his composure. "Perhaps we'll meet again at the Red Claw," he said and started to walk away.

"Where is the Red Claw?" Grey Cloak asked.

"Finding it is your first test." Tanlin left.

Grey Cloak opened the cell door, and Dyphestive followed him.

"Are we really going?" Dyphestive asked.

"I don't know." At the desk, Grey Cloak poured his coins into his hands. The silver had been replaced with worthless bits of copper. "I don't think we have a choice."

GREY CLOAK WAS SITTING ON THE FRONT EDGE OF A porch behind a trough of water where a pair of horses was drinking. Dyphestive was beside him, eating a small loaf of bread. It was all their copper chips could buy them.

"Are you sure that you don't want a bite?" Dyphestive asked.

"No," Grey Cloak said, making a face as if he had a bitter taste in his mouth.

It was early in the evening the day after they'd been imprisoned, and the sun was setting behind the building. All day long, they had been searching the entire city for the Red Claw Tavern. No such place was in sight, and they'd passed dozens of inns and taverns. They'd even asked questions of the common citizens, who didn't offer any clues.

Grey Cloak took off his right boot and rubbed his foot. A blister had started on the side of his big toe.

Dyphestive leaned over and said, "At least you are breaking your new boots in."

"Yes, that's exactly what I was thinking." He shook his head and stuffed his foot back in the boot. "It's always nice to have you point out the lighter side of our situation."

Dyphestive ripped what was left of his bread and fed it to the pair of horses. The beasts nickered and nodded.

"Why in Gapoli would you give them our last scrap of food?" Grey Cloak asked.

"You said you didn't want any." Dyphestive scratched one of the horses behind an ear. "And horses get hungry too."

"That's brilliant. Maybe they'll invite you over to their barn, and they'll share a bale of hay with you." He stood up and looked up and down the street. With his hands on his hips, he said, "We have to be missing something. How hard could it be to find the Red Claw Tavern? The name has a ring to it."

"Maybe we should circle back to Zora's store. She might be there now."

"No, we tried that once, and personally, I hate asking." He picked up a broken piece of cobblestone and skipped it across the street. "This is some sort of test. It has to be."

"We don't have to take it. We can always go and do something else."

Grey Cloak didn't hear him because his wheels were spinning. Their quest was a challenge, and he liked it.

Finally, the sun set behind the buildings, and the bustling streets were covered in the evening shade. Scratching the smooth skin on his cheeks, he said, "Come to think of it, Tanlin said to come in the evening. Maybe it's a place that can only be seen at night."

Dyphestive dug in his ear with his pinky and said, "I guess that's possible." He hefted his anvil-laden sack over his shoulder. "Lead the way."

Raven Cliff hosted more than its fair share of inns and taverns. They varied from run-down buildings to the most well-built architecture. Some of them catered to one partic-ular race, while others catered to them all. The dwarves frequented the spots that offered many spirits and dreadful songs, while the elves preferred something with more wine and refinery. Halflings and gnomes entered through doors that were their height. The orcen taverns smelled the worst.

Dyphestive covered his nose as they walked around a tavern where dark-haired orcs with flat noses and large nostrils stood outside the door, making a ruckus.

"Don't look at them," Grey Cloak said. "They only want your attention."

But Dyphestive looked right at the big-framed orcs, who were covered in hair as coarse as their language.

"Come over here, boy!" a beastly orc with strands of braided hair said. "Drink with us, little pink man!"

"No, thank you," Dyphestive replied.

"Will you be *quiet*?" Grey Cloak pushed his brother in the back, and they both picked up the pace.

"We'll be waiting for you next time, human! You, too, elf!" the orc yelled.

"You had to look, didn't you?"

"It's hard not to look at them." Dyphestive made a sour face. "I can't explain it. It makes me think of carrion that the vultures feast on."

"Yes, thanks for painting the picture in my mind." Grey Cloak hurried along with his sore feet burning and eyed every sign and building that they passed. Not a single one of the tavern signs read anything remotely close to Red Claw.

Following the warm evening breeze, they headed to the southern side of the city. Many taverns and inns overlooked a league-long cliff that gave a scenic view of the valley. Along the edge of and hanging over the one-hundred-foot-high cliff was a sturdy boardwalk. Crowds of people were walking along the boardwalk, where they were enjoying a variety of food from carts and clustering around traveling troubadours that were trying to earn some chips.

Grey Cloak picked a spot and leaned with his back against the railing, and Dyphestive joined him. They'd been looking all day long, and Grey Cloak was tired of it. "I'm starting to wonder if this *Red Claw* even exists."

"Perhaps Tanlin was only playing another trick on us. You know, to throw us off of his tail," Dyphestive replied.

"We walked through all of the alleys, didn't we?"

"I think."

Grey Cloak rifled through his thoughts. He had a keen sense of detail, and nothing they'd passed jumped out at him. He'd looked for any sign that showed a red claw or something remotely close. The mystery was eating at him. He elbowed Dyphestive. "Let's go."

Together, they traipsed down the boardwalk, weaving their way through the crowds. Dyphestive's big hands swung easily at his sides. Grey Cloak snuck by everyone, making sure that he wasn't touched. He looked back from time to time to see that his brother was keeping up. Every fifty yards, they would pass a set of stairs that led down to the fields. The stairs stayed busy with people climbing up and down, and each one had a sign mounted next to it. They all had funny names.

Dyphestive uttered the names on all of the signs as he walked by. "Zooflan Falls. The Up-and-Downer. The Place of Many Steps. Look but Don't Leap. Red Claw Tavern. Der Walc Nrevat." He scratched his head. "That's a hard one to say."

Grey Cloak stopped then walked backward and gave the Red Claw Tavern sign a calculating look. His gaze ran from left to right and right to left. He slapped Dyphestive on the back. "Red Claw Tavern."

Without hesitation, Grey Cloak and Dyphestive scuttled down the steps like a pair of hungry mice, garnering startled looks and objections from the folks they blew by. The stairs cut back and forth, with large landings every two flights. When the path was clear, Grey Cloak jumped down a flight at a time. When it wasn't, he ran down the railing like a cat, leaving his brother to fight through the crowd to catch up with him.

"Excuse me. Excuse me." Dyphestive apologized over and over on the way down. He caught up with his brother halfway to the bottom. Another deck ran along the crooked face of the cliff. "Where do we go?" he asked.

Grey Cloak squinted his steely eyes and locked them on three men who were standing outside, smoking pipes and cigars and blowing smoke over the deck railing. With the separate decking only wide enough for a few people, no one else was traversing it. "This way."

Walking east along the narrow deck, they moved on until they came to a huge cleft in the cliff. The cleft worked more like a cave, with a rock floor, and had a hand of red claws with golden talons painted on it. A set of wooden double doors with brass ring handles ominously waited for them.

A sign was posted outside the door, and Dyphestive read it. "Some are welcome. Most are not. Enter at your peril."

26

WITH A PUZZLED LOOK, DYPHESTIVE SAID, "ARE YOU sure you want to do this?"

"Of course I am." Grey Cloak cast a glance over his shoulder. The three rough-hewn men that had been smoking were gone. He grabbed the handle and yanked it, and the door groaned on rusted hinges. "So much for being subtle."

They slipped into the dimness of the Red Claw Tavern, which was more like a large cavern, though it was laid out with the same furnishings that one would typically see in a tavern. A natural chill lingered in the air. The table and chairs were made from dark maple. Over half of the seats were filled with assorted patrons. Some were engaging in robust conversation and others weren't. A perfectly circular bar was in the center of the room, and most of the barstools were full, though not a single person glanced their way. A quartet was standing on a small stage, singing quietly and plucking stringed instruments.

Grey Cloak nudged his brother with his elbow and pointed at the torches in iron brackets mounted on the cave walls. No smoke was coming from the torches. Instead, a warm orange glow was emanating from the quartz, which replaced natural flames. Flameless candles fashioned the same as the quartz torches sat on the tables, casting shadows on the faces of the strange tavern visitors.

Two humongous hands dropped down on Grey Cloak and Dyphestive's shoulders. The fingernails were large and black and bit into their shoulders, and fetid breath made them cover their noses.

Together, they looked up. An ogre was hovering over them like a shaded tree. His face was round, pitted, and ugly, and drool was dripping from his lip. The ogre's heavy stare could have pushed them to the ground. In a guttural voice, the monstrous ogre said, "You look lost."

"Er..." Grey Cloak started to say.

A man hurried over from a table at the back of the room, moving with grace and ease. It was Tanlin. "It's quite all right, Butterlip. They are with me."

"Humph," Butterlip said as he released them. He glared at Tanlin. "You need to let me know when you have company coming. Next time, I'll pitch them over the deck." He moved backward and sank into an alcove that barely fit his tremendous frame. His bright-yellow eyes could barely be seen in the dim light.

Tanlin offered a friendly smile. He was no longer wearing the well-fashioned clothing he'd worn before and had changed into something loose fitting and frumpy. The perfect waves in his hair were messy. "I knew you would make it. Well done. Let's get you seated."

They all sat down at a small round table with a keg barrel underneath being used for the leg. Grey Cloak and Dyphestive followed Tanlin's suit and leaned over the table.

He spoke quietly. "Now that you are here, I still have some convincing to do."

"What do you mean?" Grey Cloak asked.

"I work with a much larger group, and we don't take just anyone in. It doesn't help that you are so young, either." He gave each of them a glance and said, "You're young and as green as a sprout."

"We are more than ready for anything." Grey Cloak tapped his finger on the table. "I can assure you of that."

Tanlin lifted his hand and said, "Don't be so sure of yourself. We've managed to rob you three times, haven't we? But don't take offense. We were all young and stupid once."

"I'm not stupid." Grey Cloak looked around. "Where's Zora?"

Walking away, Tanlin said, "Don't worry. She'll be along. Now stay put. I'll send you over something to eat."

Dyphestive drummed his big hands on the table.

"That's the best news I've heard all day." He sniffed the air and made a curious look. "I don't smell anything cooking."

Grey Cloak wasn't paying any attention to what Dyphestive said. He was too busy watching the group of people that Tanlin had joined at the other table, but his brother's big shoulders were in the way. He waved his hand. "Will you scoot over? You're blocking my view."

Dyphestive hopped his chair over then turned and followed Grey Cloak's eyes. "Who do you think they are?"

"That's what I'm trying to find out."

Tanlin had joined two other men. They quickly engaged in a heated conversation. The men, like Tanlin, were much older than Grey Cloak and Dyphestive. One of them was a well-knit warrior wearing plate-mail armor. He had a stern countenance. The other man was dressed in midnight-blue robes with silver lining. His thick hair was long and dark, but his face was bitter and hard.

"Do you think they are talking about us?" Dyphestive asked.

"Of course they are." Grey Cloak narrowed his eyes. "Now be quiet. I'm trying to see or hear what they are saying." He had a natural knack for eavesdropping and reading lips. It had always kept him in the loop at Havenstock. He prided himself on knowing what was happening with everyone at all times and places. "A warrior, a rogue, and a wizard. Interesting."

"Well, even I can see that," Dyphestive said.

Tanlin had his back facing Grey Cloak. It didn't help that the barmaids kept passing between the tables, not to mention numerous patrons. The wizard-looking fellow was wearing an ornate ring on each ring finger. The warrior kept one hand on a dagger handle on his sword belt. He had a long mustache and gently nodded as Tanlin spoke. The crafting of his armor was some of the best that Grey Cloak had ever seen. *Who are these men?*

27

A BARMAID SET A PLATTER OF FOOD ON THE TABLE AND asked, "Are you hungry?"

Dyphestive said brightly, "Yes!" He started filling his large hands with hunks of pepper, dried meat, and squares of cheeses.

She filled up two metal goblets with red juice. "Enjoy. Is there anything else I can get you?"

"No," Grey Cloak said as he focused on the men across the room.

"Are you sure?" she said.

"I know it's you, Zora. I recognized your voice immediately, but I'm busy at the moment," he said.

"Huh?" Dyphestive gave the barmaid a closer study. "Oh, I didn't even recognize you. Something is different. Ah, it's your hair. It's pretty."

Grey Cloak glanced up at Zora. Her short auburn hair was replaced by long and shining locks that looked like they'd been dipped in honey. It hung down over her shoulders, and she was wearing a tight black vest with a cotton shirt underneath it. Her black boots covered her ankles, and a belt of daggers made a ring around her perfect hips. He swallowed and said, "My, you look—"

"Amazing," she said.

"Surprising," he answered. *And amazing. Yes. Amazing.*

Dyphestive stood up and pulled out another chair. "Please, have a seat."

Zora fanned herself with her hand and said, "Oh, I wouldn't want to interrupt anything important. Grey Garment looks very busy."

"It's Grey Cloak." He patted the tabletop. "Don't be silly. Please join us and, uh, tell us what you know about the men your father is with."

"Tanlin isn't my father." She gave a delightful laugh. "He's my mentor. You really shouldn't jump to conclusions."

"I wasn't jumping to conclusions. I was only eliminating the possibility." He gave her a quick smile.

"Of course you were," she replied. "Anyway, I'm glad you found Red Claw. It was beginning to get late, and I had my doubts."

"So who is Tanlin talking to?" Grey Cloak asked.

"That's Adanadel and Dalsay. Adanadel used to be a

knight in Monarch City. Dalsay is a member of the Wizard Watch. Or perhaps a former member. I'm not certain. The Guild of Mages is full of a bunch of odd ones." She swiped her hair over her shoulder and tied it back in a ponytail. "They've been working together for many years. They call themselves Talon."

"Like the painting in the front of the tavern?" Dyphestive asked.

"Actually, I think they named their group after that," she said.

Grey Cloak helped himself to some juicy green grapes and asked, "Are you a part of their group?"

"Yes, but I've only been on one campaign. That was almost a year ago."

Grey Cloak scooted closer to her. "A campaign?" he asked. "What sort? Lost treasure?"

"It depends. Dalsay shows up and rounds up members of the group. He's the mind behind it. The last time... well, the only time for me... we raided a tomb. Not all of us came back."

Grey Cloak sat on the edge of his seat. "What did you find?"

"Chips and gems. A couple other unique items." She glanced at Dyphestive. "Are you enjoying your food?"

"It's good. How many chips and gems?"

"Well, aren't *you* curious?" she said.

Grey Cloak put his hand on her forearm and said, "We

are both curious. It's been very difficult to keep track of our coins lately."

She tugged at his chin and said, "Don't worry. If this works out, you'll get back ten times what you lost."

"I'd better," he replied.

Tanlin threw his arms up and stormed away from the table. He marched right over to Grey Cloak, Dyphestive, and Zora. "I'm sorry, boys, but they said no. I couldn't get them to budge." He dropped a silk coin purse on the table. "This is for the trouble. Come on, Zora. Let's go. It's time to get ready."

"Wait, what happened?" Grey Cloak demanded.

Tanlin headed toward the front door, towing a sad-faced Zora behind him, and said with growing frustration in his voice, "It's out of my hands."

Grey Cloak dared a look at Adanadel and Dalsay. The pair of hard-eyed men were staring right at him. He glared back until someone bumped into his chair. It was a sloppy-looking man teetering between the tables.

"Watch out!" Grey Cloak said. When he looked back at the men's table, they were gone. "Dyphestive, did you see where they went?"

With his nose in his plate of food, Dyphestive was eating like someone might steal it from him. "Nuh-uh," he said with his mouth full.

Grey Cloak's gaze swept over the room, but he saw no sign of them. "Zooks."

28

TEN SILVER CHIPS WERE INSIDE THE PURSE THAT
Tanlin had left them. Grey Cloak stacked them up on the
table then grabbed three coins from the top of the stack and
juggled them with one hand. "I need to go after them."

"Why? They don't want us. And we are better off now
than we were before," Dyphestive said.

"Did you hear Zora? We could earn back ten times our
money. Perhaps twenty. Go on a real adventure. Doesn't
that sound good to you?"

Dyphestive shrugged. "I'll go where you go."

"I hate your chronic indifference." He continued to scan
the room for Adanadel and Dalsay. Their table was still
empty. *I know the man is a wizard, but he couldn't just
vanish, could he?*

The other odd thing was that no one else in the tavern

was startled by the sudden disappearance. The patrons were continuing to go about their business as if nothing had happened. Grey Cloak caught the coins and put them back in the purse then pulled the strings tight and tossed the small sack to Dyphestive. "Hang on to that." He pushed his chair back and got up.

"Where are you going?"

"Be still. I'm going to look around the place. Doesn't it make your hair stand up that two men vanished into thin air?"

"Yeah, but one of them is a wizard. They can do that, can't they?"

"Perhaps."

Grey Cloak sauntered through the chilly tavern. The lively band's quick fingers shredded the necks of their stringed instruments. They were two women and two men, half elven and attractive. None of them cast a glance at Grey Cloak as he walked by. *Something is not right about this place.*

He moved to Tanlin's table and put his hand on the chair where Tanlin had been sitting. The worn black wood was still warm. When he touched the chairs that Adanadel and Dalsay had sat in, his sensitive touch picked up that the chairs were cool, as if they had never been sat in before. *I don't think they were even here.* He thought of Batram the halfling... or whatever the odd trader was. He had turned into many different creatures in a blink.

Grey Cloak hustled over to Dyphestive and sat back down. "They were never there."

"What? Who wasn't there?"

"Adanadel and Dalsay. The men that Tanlin sat down and spoke with. They were never there at all. It was only an illusion."

He leaned over and poked a man in the back. The man turned and glowered at him.

"Sorry," Grey Cloak said. "I was making sure you were real."

"Oh, I'm real. Real agitated. Mind your business, elf." The man turned around and hunkered over his drink again.

The slob that had bumped into Grey Cloak earlier grabbed a chair from their table, turned it around, and sat down. He was a man of decent size and not very handsome, and he looked to have some orc in him. He had big hips and legs that seemed out of place with his body. Looking Grey Cloak and Dyphestive dead on, he made a sucking sound out of the corner of his mouth and said, "You figured it out."

Dyphestive stopped eating.

Grey Cloak brightened. "I was right. It was an illusion."

"It was a test. *You* passed it. They call me Browning." He rubbed his neck. "I'm a member of Talon. Been keeping an eye on you since you've been here." He grabbed a goblet from the table and drank, but he spat it out. "What is this poison?" Making a sour face, he wiped his mouth, then he shouted at the bartender, "Gertie! Get me something

fermented over here! Yuk, I can't stand that sweet stuff."
Browning had an obnoxious but friendly way about him
and a knack for talking out of the side of his mouth. "I like
the bitters."

Grey Cloak asked, "Are Adanadel and Dalsay real?"

"Aye. They are real."

A barmaid brought a tankard of ale over and set it on
the table.

Browning smacked her on the rear end, winked at her,
and said, "Thanks, darlin'." He gulped down the entire
tankard and slammed it on the table. "Ah, that's better." He
eyed Grey Cloak and said, "Do you have many
belongings?"

"Only what I have with me."

"Good." Browning stood up, and his chair legs scraped
across the floor. "Let's go then."

Grey Cloak and Dyphestive came to their feet.

Browning eyed Dyphestive and said, "Sorry, but I'm
only taking the elf. Not you."

29

"Where he goes, I go," Dyphestive argued. "We're brothers!"

Browning lifted an eyebrow and said, "Pardon?"

"Blood brothers. And you can't separate us," Dyphestive replied.

"Boy, I don't care what sort of brother you are, but the elf impressed. You didn't. All you did was sit down on your duff and eat. We're in a tavern full of people that can do that."

"But—"

Grey Cloak stepped in front of his brother and said, "I can assure you that my brother is more than resourceful. He's as strong as an ox." He patted Dyphestive's thick arms. "And as loyal as a hound. Certainly, you have a use for him."

Browning gave Dyphestive a casual up-and-down glance and asked, "Do you even own a weapon?"

Dyphestive set his sack filled with a small anvil on the table and said, "I have this."

"Let me see that." Browning snatched the sack out of Dyphestive's grip, opened it, and looked inside. "Is that an anvil?" His gaze slid between them. "Who in Great Circle carries an anvil around?" He put his hands on his belly and clucked with laughter.

"We're blacksmiths," Dyphestive said with a sheepish look. "It's a keepsake."

Browning stopped laughing and said, "You're hauling around forty pounds of steel as a keepsake." He burst out laughing again then dropped to his knees and pounded on the table. Finally, he regained his composure and stood up. "I imagine you have a spine as hard as iron, but in your case, you need to know how to fight. Strength isn't worth a cow's lick if you can't use it."

"I can fight," Dyphestive said.

Browning's voice became gravelly, and his eyes narrowed. "Is that so? Well, let's find out. Gertie! Clear the tables! It's time for a match."

No sooner had the tables moved than the crowd was on their feet in an excited frenzy. A ring formed around Browning and Dyphestive, and women climbed on men's shoulders and hollered with jubilation. Grey Cloak stood in the front of the throng, eyeing Browning's every move.

Browning rolled up the sleeves of his jerkin. He was taller than Dyphestive, big-boned, and soft in the midsection, but he moved with panther-like ease. He wasn't carrying a weapon that could be seen, but his hands, wrists, and knuckles were thick with calluses.

"Put your hand up here, boy," Browning said as he spread his fingers wide and held up his hand. Dyphestive's hand was noticeably bigger.

"Goodness, looks like you got some ogre in you!" Browning said.

Chortles erupted in the room.

"Listen, boy, this ain't a wrestling match. It's a fistfight. I need to see what you have in you." Browning hit his belly with his fist. "Don't hold back, either, cause I won't. Understand?"

Dyphestive glanced at Grey Cloak and nodded.

"Good. Now ball those sledgehammers up and get them up," Browning said. "Ready?"

"Ready."

Browning punched Dyphestive in the mouth. *Crack.* Dyphestive's head snapped back, and he stumbled backward. When he touched his lip, his fingers came away bloody. The crowd roared, and Grey Cloak winced.

Browning marched forward and unloaded a flurry of heavy punches. His meaty fists collided with hard flesh. *Whap! Whap! Whomp!* He hit belly, shoulder, chest, and chin with hammer-like punches. Dyphestive started to block the punches with his hands up like crab claws then bulled forward and unleashed an uppercut.

Browning slid his chin out of the way and peppered Dyphestive's face with stiff jabs. "Is that what you call fighting? Getting hit?"

"No. I call this fighting." He charged the older man and unleashed a succession of haymakers. His fist beat wildly into Browning's shoulders and pounded on his back. *Thump! Thump! Thump!*

Browning tied up Dyphestive and spoke in his ear. "In the real world, you would be dead now, boy. You're going to have to do better than that." He pushed him away, got his guard up, and lowered his shoulders. He ducked under two hard swings from Dyphestive then landed a right hook on his jaw.

A tooth flew out of Dyphestive's mouth, and he took a step back and gave a wide grin. One of his top teeth was missing. Still, he advanced. The throng of people threw up their arms and cheered.

Dyphestive and Browning exchanged a series of hard blows. Browning's superior skill landed five punches to Dyphestive's one, but both of them started puffing and panting, and sweat dripped from their faces.

Browning faded away then snaked in and peppered Dyphestive's face with an onslaught of punches. Dyphestive pushed the man back and beckoned him with his fists.

"You're going to wish you hadn't done that." Browning landed jab after jab and finished with a hard body blow that bent Dyphestive half over, then he struck his exposed jaw.

Dyphestive staggered around the ring on wobbly legs for three large steps.

"He's going down!" someone screamed.

Grey Cloak urged his brother on. "Stay up, Dy! Stay up!"

Dyphestive stopped, straightened his back, and lifted his fists.

Browning groaned and said, "You're a glutton for punishment. So be it." He began wailing on him.

They fought toe-to-toe, neither giving the other quarter as they pounded away at one another. Dyphestive cocked back and unleashed a powerful punch to Browning's belly.

Air exploded out of the man's mouth. "Oof!"

The crowd gave a loud "Ooh!"

Browning locked onto Dyphestive and squeezed him tight, panting in his ear. "Have you had enough?"

"Not even close," Dyphestive said.

"Good." Browning pushed him away. "But we're done here, boy. We're done." He patted his fist on the back of Dyphestive's head. "Well done."

Dyphestive nodded and said, "So I can come."

Browning nodded, broke away, and said, "What's done is done. The fight's over. I hope you folks enjoyed it."

The dejected crowd made comments of disappointment as they dragged their tables and chairs back into place.

Browning slumped into his seat, holding his stomach, and said, "Gertie. More bitters." He eyed Dyphestive and Grey Cloak. "Sit down and join me."

30

Dusk had begun to settle, making the clear skies awash with purple and blue. Farmers were coming in from the fields, some fanning themselves with their large straw hats. A herd of cows trampled over the road, stirring up dust, as the shepherd dogs nipped at their tails.

Grey Cloak spit the dust from his mouth. He and Dyphestive had been following Browning on an hours-long walk, traipsing the roads that led south away from Raven Cliff and toward the Iron Hills. Browning walked with a jumpy gait because he had a small hitch in his step, and he talked a lot.

"Listen, boys. When we get there, keep your mouths shut. I'll have to handle Dalsay and Adanadel. They won't be pleased that I'm bringing the big one along." He rubbed his shoulder. "Durn, you can hit, boy." He gave Dyphestive a curious look. "If you can learn to hit what you aim for, you'll be dangerous one day."

"I *am* dangerous," Dyphestive commented. His face was swollen, but he walked easily, with his arms swinging at his sides.

"You don't know dangerous," Browning said. He was wearing a sword belt and carrying a small round buckler. "You don't want to see it, but you will eventually."

"I can't wait," Grey Cloak said. He moved alongside Browning. "What sort of adventure are we going to be going on?"

Browning lifted a finger. "First, you'll only know what you are told and do as you're told. Don't push Adanadel or Dalsay. They are short-tempered." He gave an ugly grin. "They aren't as charming as me." A goat ran right by him, almost knocking him over, and he kicked at it. "Durn animals! Watch where you're going!" He wiped his sweat away on his sleeve. "Where was I?"

"You were telling me about Dalsay," Dyphestive said.

"Ah yes. Dalsay. Well, you know, he's one of those wizards and spends his time searching through those big books. I forget what you call them."

"Tomes?" Dyphestive suggested.

"Spell books," Grey Cloak added.

"Something like that. Anyway, he does his weird thing and rounds us up, and we go and look for it." He stopped and stretched, nearly hitting Dyphestive and Grey Cloak in the chest with his buckler. "But don't ask him about it. If there is anything he hates, it's trying to pry into his big head." He resumed his pace.

"I see. So we are seeking treasure, aren't we?" Grey Cloak asked.

Browning spat. "I'm not trying to get myself killed for nothing. I'm mostly in it for the gold, but according to Dalsay and Adanadel, we serve the greater good of Gapoli too. And I'm all right with that."

The old warrior led them through the farm village to a spot in the tall grasses where many stone cottages were covered in overgrowth. A stream of smoke came out of one of the cottages' chimneys.

Browning made a strange clicking sound, like he was calling a horse, with his mouth and pointed at the cottage with the chimney smoke. "I'm going in there." He pointed at a dogwood tree. "The two of you get over there and plant your fannies on those roots. I mean it when I say don't move."

They nodded and sat down, and Browning crossed through the grasses, knocked on the wooden door, and quickly went inside.

Grey Cloak stood up and headed for the cottage.

"What are you doing?" Dyphestive asked. He was rubbing the spot where his front tooth was missing.

"I'm going to go and have a listen."

"Of course you are." Dyphestive found an onion stem in

the grass and gently pulled it out. The onion bulb was as big as his thumb. "And I'll have something to eat."

Grey Cloak sneaked over to the cottage and took a knee beside the door. The wind rustled over the grasses. He brushed his hair behind his ear and put his ear to the door.

"You brought them both?" someone said in a stern voice that carried the bitterness of a chill wind. "We only wanted the elf."

Grey Cloak assumed Dalsay was talking, but he wasn't sure. It could have been Adanadel.

"No," Browning argued, "you said to test them both. To find worthiness. I did that. I'm telling you the boy is plenty worthy. I hit him with everything I had. He's got a face made of stone, and I had to pop my little finger back into joint. Look at my hands. They're swelling."

"I like them both," Tanlin injected.

"So do I," said Zora. "Dyphestive is strong. We can never have enough strong backs."

"This mission isn't about hauling out coffers of coin," someone else said with a stern voice that was also mannerly and distinguished. "It carries greater weight than that."

Grey Cloak could visualize the warrior that Tanlin had spoken with inside the Red Claw Tavern—the man in armor. Armor softly creaked when the person spoke, and Grey Cloak assumed it was Adanadel.

"But there will be spoils to be gained, right?" Tanlin said.

"There are always spoils," Dalsay said, "but not at the expense of this mission. The only reason I am considering the elf is because of what you told me about the hermit. I don't brush off those stories as a coincidence. I was trained better than that. Every bizarre incidence can have meaning."

Everyone else in the room sarcastically replied, "*We know.*"

Grey Cloak covered his mouth and fought back a giggle. He could have sworn he heard another voice among them that he couldn't identify. *Is there someone else in there? Possibly two?*

"We will take it to a vote. A simple majority wins," Dalsay said. "I vote no. Adanadel votes no. Tanlin, yes. Zora, yes. Browning, yes."

Grey Cloak pumped his fist. *That's a majority.*

"Tatiana," Dalsay said in a strict voice, "remember, in the event of a tie, the brute remains. What is your vote?"

Grey Cloak bit down on his knuckle. *Oh no.*

31

Silence lingered in the stone cottage. Grey
Cloak could envision the group staring at the mysterious
Tatiana. His mind raced. *Who is she? She sounds very
pretty.*

Dalsay gave a noticeable sigh. "Tatiana votes yes. That's
a majority."

The cottage door swung open.

Grey Cloak was on one knee, grinning with surprise.
He wiggled his fingers. "Uh, hello." He rose out of his
crouch. "I guess I can come in now."

Dalsay was sitting at the head of a wooden table, facing
the entrance. The hawkish wizard's eyes were locked on
Grey Cloak. He was wearing black robes mixed with gray
in a flowing checkered pattern. The hems of his sleeves
were trimmed in gold. There was no mistaking the irritation

on his face. To Dalsay's right was Adanadel. The stone-faced warrior was as he'd appeared before, wearing a well-crafted suit of plate mail armor. Tanlin, Zora, and Browning were standing around the table with victorious smiles warming their faces.

Sitting on Dalsay's left was a full-blood elf that Grey Cloak had not seen before—Tatiana. Underneath locks of caramel-colored hair was an angelic face as warm as the sun, and she had enchanting lavender eyes that could take a man's breath away. Her body was wrapped in butter-and-cinnamon-colored robes. The expression on her face couldn't have been more inviting. Grey Cloak's mouth dried as he opened it to introduce himself.

Dalsay's eyebrows knitted. "Go away!"

The door slammed with jarring impact right in Grey Cloak's face. He hurried back to Dyphestive, who was leaning against the tree with his eyes closed and his fingers locked together over his chest.

"Well? Did they kick me out yet?" Dyphestive asked without budging.

"No, we are in!"

Dyphestive opened an eye. "Really?"

"Yes, and there is another elf. A full blood like me. She is a vision. Old but still a vision."

Dyphestive sat up and asked, "How old?"

"You know, like the others, except Zora, of course."

"So what do we do now?"

Grey Cloak looked at the cottage. "I don't know. Maybe they'll make us swear a secret oath or something."

"Do you really think they will do that?"

He shrugged. "I'm sure it will be something good."

They sat quietly for over an hour. Finally, the cottage door opened, and Browning came out and closed the door behind him. He waved them over and said, "Come with me."

GREY CLOAK and Dyphestive hoofed it through the Iron Hills with heavy packs of gear on their backs. They marched through hard rain to the top of the hills.

Grey Cloak's back burned, and his feet throbbed. The rain hadn't stopped since the first day. He looked behind him at Dyphestive and said, "This almost makes me miss Rhonna."

Dyphestive managed a goofy grin as he trucked up the hillside like a mountain goat. "At least we are getting fed."

"Hah. All we get is rice and beans. And we have to cook it all," he said.

They were in the rear of the group, carrying the heaviest loads. Dalsay had insisted that they didn't speak unless spoken to, which Grey Cloak had reluctantly obeyed.

"It might not be so bad if this rain would stop. We don't even know where we're going."

"The rain doesn't bother me, but I would like to know where we were going." Dyphestive slipped on a moss-covered rock and went crashing down the hillside twenty feet before he stopped.

The entire party stopped and looked down at him.

Grey Cloak glared back at them and said, "Don't everybody move at once." He hurried down the hill and helped Dyphestive back to his feet.

"Thanks," Dyphestive said. He started the march back up the hill again.

"Well, quit falling down. This is the third time."

"It's slippery."

"And noisy." Zora had made her way down the hillside. Unlike Dyphestive and Grey Cloak, she wasn't carrying a heavy pack of any sort. Instead, she was draped in a cloak that covered her body and shed water like a duck. "We aren't alone in these dangerous hills."

"We know," Grey Cloak said. He hopped over a deep groove that made a natural channel of water down the hill and stood by her. He gave her garment a pinch. "Nice cloak. Did you steal it?"

"Maybe."

She looked up the hill. Dalsay and Adanadel were looking right down on them like vultures. They turned their backs and started walking.

"Let's keep moving. You're slowing us down."

"It's not me. It's him," he said.

"I'm moving just as fast as anyone else," Dyphestive argued. "We'll be fine." He slipped on another moss-covered stone and landed hard on his knee. "I'm fine." He got up and came after them.

Zora started to hurry back up the hill.

Grey Cloak caught her by the elbow. "Zora, I thought we were a part of Talon. Not its slaves."

Zora pulled away. "We all have to contribute one way or another. Besides, you don't have any weapons. What else can you do?"

Dyphestive hollered up the hill, "I have an anvil. And I don't mind carrying things. I'm good at it."

"I can see that," she said. "And I thank you. But don't cross Dalsay. He's very serious and impatient."

Grey Cloak gave her an annoyed look. "Can't you at least tell me where we are going?"

"I would love to, but even I don't know that. Only Dalsay and Adanadel do."

Dumbfounded, he said, "Are you serious?"

"As serious as a warlock."

"Are you referring to Dalsay?"

"In his dreams." She gave him a curious glance and said, "You seem awfully familiar with certain terminology. Have you always been a farmhand?"

He shrugged and gave her a misleading answer. "I pick up on things. Besides, I've been to Portham many times before."

"Uh-huh. I see. You know, you were chosen because I felt—well, Tanlin and I both felt that there was more to you than meets the eye. Don't try to make a fool out of him." She hurried up the hill and caught up with the rest of the group.

Down the hill, Dyphestive was giving Grey Cloak a knowing look. Grey Cloak put a finger to his lips and said, "Shh."

A sharp whistle came from high up on the hill. Zora feverishly waved at them to hide, then she vanished into the trees.

Grey Cloak and Dyphestive burrowed in the brush.

From his vantage point, Grey Cloak couldn't see the others through the foliage. Instead, he heard something large pushing through the brush higher up the hill. He parted the brush and got a glimpse of a wiry knot of bodies pushing through the rain. He whispered to Dyphestive, "Goblins."

One of the goblins was bigger than the rest, standing over nine feet tall.

Dyphestive swallowed loudly and said, "Giant goblins."

32

THE GOBLINS WERE WIRY LITTLE MEN CARRYING SPEARS and hatchets. Necklaces made from small bones rattled over their dirty bodies. They had shifty yellow eyes and sniffed like wild hounds.

Among them was a giant compared to the others of their kind. His jet-black hair was tied up in a knot on the top of his head, and his close-set eyes were beady. His nose was pierced with a bone, his belly hung over his belt, and he was lugging a huge iron sword over his shoulder as he traversed the hills on huge feet. Behind him, he was dragging a net full of gnomes.

Grey Cloak's breath caught in his throat. The goblins chortled gleefully as they poked and prodded the gnomes, who were snarling in the giant's net. The gnomes were thick little men with coarse beards that came to a point over their chests. Their stubby fingers strained at the nets they were tangled in.

"What do we do?" Dyphestive whispered. "We can't let them take those gnomes."

"I don't know. I'm not in charge here." Grey Cloak didn't know a lot about gnomes, but he didn't want to see them eaten, not by goblins or anyone else. He eyed the giant's sword. It was big enough to hew an oak. He felt Dyphestive stirring beside him, but he kept his eyes fixed on the approaching goblins and said, "Be still."

"I have to do something."

"You can't fight that thing. He's huge. And you don't even have a weapon," Grey Cloak argued.

Dyphestive shimmied off his backpack and held out his sack and anvil. "I have this."

"Don't you dare!" Grey Cloak whispered harshly.

But Dyphestive pulled free of his grip and ventured onto the muddy path in the spitting rain. He started to spin the sack and anvil like a sling and stone and shouted up the hill, "Release the gnomes!"

The goblins let out a wild cry filled with elation then sank into a crouch and beat their weapons on the rocks. They pointed at Dyphestive, clacked their teeth, and spewed fiendish chatter.

The giant gave a broad grin showing busted teeth and rotting flesh hanging between them. He let go of the net and held out his sword. It was a two-handed weapon made for men, but the goblin carried it easily in one hand. He beat his chest and shouted, "Human want gnomes! Human take gnomes!"

Dyphestive spun the anvil in the sack with all of his might and let the crude weapon fly.

The goblins' eyes followed the missile sailing over their heads. The anvil collided with the giant's chest—*Thunk!* —and fell to the ground.

The giant's face darkened. A heavy growl started to build in his throat. "I felt that! I didn't like it!" He brushed his huge crooked fingers over his chest. "You will pay!" He pointed his sword at Dyphestive. "Brothers! Bring that succulent human to me!"

A bright flash of lightning lit up the hills in blinding white light, and a bolt of energy ripped through the giant goblin's chest. He threw his arms out wide, his jaw hung open, and he shook like a tree in a storm. As his sword fell from his fingers, smoke billowed out of his mouth and eyes, and his burning hair singed his skin. He fell forward and died.

The goblins stood around their fallen leader with their jaws dropped. Quickly, their shock turned to rage. They set their burning yellow eyes on Dyphestive, raised their axes, and lowered their spears.

Adanadel and Browning burst out of the rocky woodland hills with their swords flashing, and a goblin's head leapt from his shoulders thanks to the quickness of

Adanadel's striking sword. Browning shoved his steel through two goblins at once then smote another one in the jaw with his fist and put him to death with his sword.

Grey Cloak absorbed every devastating chop, slice, parry, and cut the two older warriors made. Goblin blood ran over the rocks and quickly mixed with rain. In less than a minute, the fight was over. He moved out of his hiding spot and stood beside his brother. Higher on the hill, Dalsay and Tatiana emerged, and Tanlin and Zora were behind them.

Dalsay's knuckles glowed with fire. He pointed at Grey Cloak and Dyphestive and said in a thunderous voice, "You idiots!"

33

THE COMPANY CALLED TALON SETTLED AT THE southern base of the Iron Hills late in the evening. Grey Cloak warmed his hands over a small campfire. He and Dyphestive had been breaking their backs since they started camp. They'd unpacked and set up the tents, started the fires, and cooked the beans and rice. No one else in the company had said a word to them since they fought off the goblins and freed the gnomes.

Dyphestive dug a small spoon into a meager bowl of beans and rice. He scraped the spoon along the inside, ate up, and licked the bowl clean. Looking into his bowl he said, "Do you think they'll let me have any more?"

"After what you did today, I would say that you are lucky that they let you eat anything."

"I did the right thing, didn't I?"

Grey Cloak pulled his cloak tighter over his shoulders and shrugged.

With a frown, Dyphestive scooted back against a tree that had fallen. The iron sword the giant goblin had carried rested against the branches. He lay the sword across his lap, took a stone from the ground, and started sharpening the sword's edges.

Twenty yards away, the other members of the company were gathered over a larger campfire and talking quietly. Only Dalsay wasn't present. He had retreated immediately to his tent after it was set up.

Adanadel looked over his shoulder at Grey Cloak and Dyphestive then pitched his drink into the fire and sauntered their way.

Grey Cloak reached over and tapped Dyphestive's leg. Dyphestive glanced up, saw Adanadel, and rose to his feet. Grey Cloak stood as well. He'd never spoken with Adanadel. The seasoned warrior seemed to be the sort of person that kept people at arm's length. He carried himself with an air about him, as if he knew better than everyone else.

"You two did a foolish thing today," Adanadel stated as he gave them both a hard look.

"Me? I didn't jump out and take on the goblins," Grey Cloak argued. "I tried to stop him. Didn't I?" He looked at his brother.

Dyphestive nodded. "I was headstrong, but I did the

right thing. Those gnomes were in danger."

Adanadel placed his hands on the pommels of his sword and dagger then walked over to Dyphestive, looked into his eyes, and said, "Is that so? You saved the quarry gnomes, did you? If you saved those, how about you go and save them all?"

Dyphestive swallowed and said, "What do you mean?"

"I'll tell you what I mean." Adanadel grabbed Dyphestive's chin and turned it toward the stark outline of mountainous hills. "Those are the Iron Hills. The goblins and the gnomes have been feuding in those hills for centuries. Their affairs are not our business. Now, we've killed a goblin chieftain. What do you think is going to happen? Do you think the thousands of goblins that reside in those hills will not discover that?"

Dyphestive shrugged.

"At least the gnomes will be happy?" Grey Cloak said.

Adanadel let go of Dyphestive's chin and faced Grey Cloak. "Is that so, elf? Am I to take it that you've had numerous encounters with quarry gnomes? That you understand their ways? Perhaps they will invite us into their thriving abodes burrowed in the hills, where men who venture in never leave."

"We aren't children that can be frightened by nighttime fairy tales," he replied.

Adanadel gave Grey Cloak a fiery look. "If you are not going to follow our lead, then depart now. I'm sure that the goblins and gnomes will be more accommodating in the Iron Hills." He walked away, passed the others huddled by the campfire, and vanished inside his tent.

Dyphestive sank to his seat. The night winds howled wildly down from the Iron Hills. "Did I make a mistake?" he muttered.

Grey Cloak agreed with Adanadel, but he wasn't going to let Adanadel chew on his brother. He didn't know the man, but Adanadel didn't know them, either.

Zora made her way over to them. Her footfalls were silent as they pressed the soft grasses.

"Did you come over here to lecture us too?" Grey Cloak asked.

Dyphestive started sharpening his sword again.

"No," Zora said as she crouched over the fire. "I heard every word Adanadel said. You should feel honored. He said more to you in one evening than he has ever said to me." She flashed a smile at them both. "Don't worry. It will be all right. You live and learn."

Dyphestive ran his stone across the sword then looked at her and asked, "So you think I did the wrong thing too?"

"Your actions could have brought harm to all of us. Think about it this way... Would you rather that one of *us* died or one of those filthy quarry gnomes?"

Dyphestive's lips twitched from side to side.

"And," she added, "would you have done the same if you hadn't had the rest of us to back you up? Do you think you and your brother could have handled the goblins by yourself? You placed us all in danger."

Grey Cloak touched her arms and said, "I wouldn't want anything ever to happen to you."

"Oh please." She gently brushed his hand aside. "You definitely don't have your mind in the right place. But I suggest that you figure it out soon. That battle in the hills put a strain on Dalsay. He doesn't care for that. He has to store his energy. Try not to foul anything else up in the coming days." She stood up. "Understand?"

"Do you even know where we are going?" Grey Cloak asked.

"I told you I didn't."

"That's not a definitive answer."

Zora twirled her finger in the air and walked away.

Grey Cloak lay down on his side, smiling, and picked some wild daisies from among the grasses. He sniffed one and said, "I think she likes me." Then he plucked off one petal at a time. "I *know* she likes me."

Browning approached. His big fists rested on his wide hips. Talking out of the side of his mouth, he said, "I bet you'll never guess who gets to stand watch all night tonight."

Dyphestive nodded and stood. He lifted his sword and rested it on his shoulders.

Browning eyed the sword and said, "That's a pretty big sword. Too bad you don't have the brains to match it."

34 HAVENSTOCK

Rʜᴏɴɴᴀ ᴘᴏᴜɴᴅᴇᴅ ʜᴇʀ ʙʟᴀᴄᴋsᴍɪᴛʜ ʜᴀᴍᴍᴇʀ ᴏɴ ᴀ length of steel. Her precise blows heated and flattened the hard metal. Over the past few days, she'd broken away from the mundane routines of her craft, such as banging out horseshoes and repairing tools used in the fields. She was making a dagger with a longer blade than normal but with a handle that would fit her hand. She lifted the blade with her tongs and eyeballed the keen edge. "Hoofcham," she muttered.

She set the blade aside, took off her mitts, and headed outside. The morning breeze cooled her face, and she helped herself to some water by drinking from a ladle in the bucket. "Ah, it's not ale, but it will have to do."

It was midmorning, and most of the workers were busy

in the fields. Things were a lot quieter outside of Haven-stock without Grey Cloak and Dyphestive around.

Griff, the part orc and part ogre, appeared, running toward her and scattering the chickens he passed. He was puffing for breath when he arrived, and he bent over and put his oversized hands on his knees.

"What in the kingdoms had you running?" Rhonna asked. "I don't think I've ever seen you run before. Though that wasn't much of a run. You move more like a wounded horse."

Griff grabbed the bucket of water and drank greedily then tossed the bucket aside and wiped his forearm across his mouth. He caught his breath and said, "Doom Riders."

"What?"

He pointed west beyond the barns. She narrowed her eyes. A line of riders on beasts was approaching.

A chill went through her bones. "It can't be."

"It is. I caught a glimpse of them coming when I was hauling lumber up into the top of my barn. I'm glad I did, or they would have stolen up on me." Griff took a deep breath and slowly let it out. "What do you think they want in Havenstock?"

"Nothing good. Maybe they are only passing through."

Griff shook his head then popped his knuckles and started to pluck the hairs from them.

"Quit doing that." She slapped his hands. "They

wouldn't want anything to do with a couple of village blacksmiths."

"You know the saying. They say that where they go, death follows."

"On a sunny day like this? I doubt it." She walked over to the bucket and picked it up. "Act naturally."

"I'm going to hide," Griff said.

She lifted an eyebrow. "You? Hide? That's a really bad idea. Put on an apron and act like you're doing something."

Griff hurried into the forge, put on a leather apron, grabbed a hammer, then snagged a horseshoe and began tapping it on top of the anvil.

"Subtle. Real subtle." Rhonna took the bucket to the well and hauled the bucket down, then slowly, hand over hand, she brought the bucket back up.

The livestock suddenly hurried back into the barns, the sheep in the corrals started to whine, and the horses in the stables whinnied and nickered.

A chill went down Rhonna's back when her gaze landed on the approaching group of men. Her throat tightened at the sight of the beasts they were riding on. They weren't horses but a different breed of creature called gourns. From a distance, a casual glance wouldn't detect much of a difference between a horse and a gourn. The creatures were built the same—tall and powerful and walking on four legs—but they were vastly different.

Gourns had the heads of dragons with small horns on the top. They had demonic eyes and hot, fetid breath, and their bodies were covered in scales, giving them natural armor. Instead of hooves in the front, they had claws and talons. A serpentine tail lashed back and forth behind their backs, and their stride was long and quiet.

Rhonna counted four riders on the gourns. She'd seen their likes before and would never forget it. The Doom Riders had left an impression that would be etched in her mind forever.

The three riders in the front formed a tip of the spear. They were wearing masks painted like skulls over their faces, their bodies were covered in realistic scale armor, and they were carrying bows, swords, axes, and spears. Their mounts were loaded with quivers of arrows and campaign gear. Each of the riders was well built and came with their own unique arsenal. Their skull masks, made from leather, were dyed deep green, red, and blue.

The group stopped several yards from the well. All eyes were on Rhonna, both beast and men. The rider in the rear moved to the front. An extraordinary woman sat in the gourn's saddle. She was wearing no mask. Her hair was as white as snow. She had strong and handsome features, and a patch covered her left eye. Her armor was unlike the heavy scale worn by the others. Instead, she was wearing a suit of black leather armor, fit perfectly to her athletic frame like a second skin. Her lone bare sun-bronzed arm was lean and muscular. The other arm was covered in mail. She looked down and said, "We meet again, Rhonna."

35

GRIFF DROPPED SOMETHING INSIDE THE FORGE, making a loud clatter.

Rhonna managed to break her stare from the woman dismounting her gourn. She took a few steps backward and caught her breath. "Drysis, is it you?"

"You seem very surprised to see me," Drysis said.

Rhonna studied the woman. Drysis was carrying a specially made crossbow, and four bolts were loaded into it using a rotating mechanism. It had a pump lever on the bottom of the body that pulled the string back to fire the bolts in rapid succession. It was one-of-a-kind weapon, and Rhonna had seen it in use before.

Finally, Rhonna straightened her back and asked, "So, you're a Doom Rider now?"

"The gourns are much more fun to ride than the horses." Drysis helped herself to a drink of water using the ladle in the bucket. She licked her lips and studied the rural surroundings. "It appears that you have been doing well."

"I manage," Rhonna said. She knew Drysis from over ten years back. They had campaigned together in the Orcen Wars of Green Ridge. Drysis had led heavy cavalry and was one of the best horse riders in the land. Rhonna had been a foot soldier and a blacksmith too. She'd shod many of Drysis's horses back in the day. "I see you are keeping interesting company."

"Yes, I always liked to keep things interesting. You know that." She looked back at her men. "And the Brothers of Destruction certainly do keep it interesting." She casually leaned against the well and propped her crossbow against it. "The heat. I never get used to it."

"Yes, I always thought you were one to prefer the north. What brings you so far south these days?"

"I'm looking for some people." Drysis peeled off one of her leather riding gauntlets and fanned herself. "A pair of striplings. A boy and an elf. They would be about fifteen seasons now."

Rhonna couldn't believe her ears. Her stomach started to knot. And she was the kind of dwarf where nothing shook her guts. *She must be talking about Grey Cloak and Dyphestive. What would she want with them?* "I bring in many youths to work the fields. They don't last long."

"Do you have an elf with jet-black hair and a strapping straw-headed boy? If so, I would like to see them."

"I don't have any striplings such as that," she said, relieved that Drysis hadn't asked a spot-on question.

"Have you seen two boys like that? I was told by some of the local ilk that they'd seen two boys such as that."

Rhonna felt herself shrink underneath Drysis's commanding presence. "Uh..."

Drysis picked up her crossbow. Her polite voice began to sour when she said, "Don't try to lie to me. You know that dwarves are horrible liars."

A clatter erupted inside the forge. It sounded like a rack of weapons had fallen over. Drysis marched in, and Rhonna followed her.

Griff was on his hands and knees, picking up a pile of old weapons. "Sorry, sorry," he said in a very stupid-sounding manner. "I'm a clumsy fool. I'll fix it."

"Who is this?" Drysis asked.

"Griff," Rhonna replied.

"I see. He looks like an old warrior to me."

"One that has had too many blows to the head," Rhonna said.

She gazed outside. The Doom Riders had dismounted and were leading their beasts to the barn. The horses in the barn began to neigh and pounded their hooves against the stable walls. She hurried out of the forge and asked, "What are they doing?"

"The gourn are hungry. Don't worry, dear Rhonna. You will be fully compensated for your loss." Drysis laid a hand on Rhonna's shoulder. "Consider it a favor to an old friend."

The four gourns' sharp teeth gnashed together. They lowered their serpentine frames and slunk into the barns. The Doom Riders locked them inside, and the barnyard fell silent for a moment. The morning breezed halted. Suddenly, the barn walls shook. Wood popped and cracked. Chickens and small hogs squeezed underneath the barn's planks and raced as far away as they could. The horses' frantic neighing fell silent, and the breeze picked back up.

Drysis led Rhonna back into the forge. "Now, what were you telling me about the boy and the elf? When did you see them?"

"I didn't say I did," Rhonna said. She would rather die than give them up.

Drysis pushed Rhonna against the wall then lifted her by the neck. Griff came to his feet, and with her other hand, Drysis aimed her crossbow at his chest.

With her finger on the trigger, she said, "Get down on the ground, or I put a hole in you." She turned her attention back to Rhonna and squeezed her neck tighter. "As for you, old friend, I serve Black Frost now. He demands answers. Lift up my patch. Lift it!"

Rhonna flipped up the patch covering Drysis's left eye, which burned like a bright pink-gemstone in the light and bored straight into her soul.

"I'll make this easy on you, Rhonna. I will use the Eye of Sight, gifted to me by Black Frost, and you will tell me what I need to know without harming your dwarven pride," Drysis said. "Have you seen two boys, an elf and a man? They go by the names Dindae and Festive."

In Drysis's eye, Rhonna could see the two boys that had showed up at her farm years ago. The names didn't match, but the faces did. She didn't want to tell the truth, but the Eye of Sight pulled the words right out of her mouth. "Yes. Yes, I have." More information gushed forth. "They came here long ago. But they fled, over a week ago. I've not searched for them. I've no idea where they went."

The pink fire in Drysis's eye went out. She dropped Rhonna to the floor and flipped her eye patch down. "Show me where they slept."

Rhonna went to the small quarters in the barn where the striplings had slept. Only their two shabby blankets were left.

Drysis picked up the blankets and asked, "They slept with these?"

"I believe so." Rhonna's hands trembled. She couldn't stop shaking. It felt like her mind had been turned inside out.

"It will do." Drysis tossed the blankets to the Doom Rider in the yellow mask. "Fetch the gourns." She turned back to Rhonna and put the crossbow to her head. "I like you, Rhonna. If I didn't, I would kill you for trying to deceive me. Your service to me will not be forgotten." She turned the crossbow away and pointed at Griff, who was standing in front of the forge. "As for your assistant, I admit that I don't care for him."

She squeezed the trigger, and the crossbow bolt hit Griff in the chest and buried itself deep. Griff dropped to his knees.

Drysis pumped the handle on her crossbow, rotating the bolts, took aim, and shot Griff in the shoulder. She pumped the handle once more and shot him one last time, leaving only one of the four bolts remaining. "I always keep one loaded, just in case."

The Doom Riders led their gourns out of the barn, and the scaly beasts' snouts were smeared with blood. The frightening group climbed into their saddles and rode east, leaving a cloud of dust behind them.

Rhonna raced over to Griff and propped his head in her lap. His breath was labored.

"Rhonna," he gasped. "Don't worry about me. Find the striplings. You have to find the strip—" His eyelids fluttered. His big body stiffened, and he let out a ragged sigh and collapsed.

"Dwarves don't cry," she sniveled. "Dwarves don't cry."

36 CROW VALLEY

TWO DAYS AFTER THE GOBLIN FIGHT, THE COMPANY called Talon arrived in the bleak lands of Crow Valley, south of Red Bone. The hot sun beat down on a cracked and dusty land where the color green was scarce. They ventured into a small town on the northern outskirts of the barren valley.

Zora escorted Grey Cloak through the town, searching for supplies and gear. In a general store, she dropped some rope and some torch sticks on the counter, and he dropped sacks of beans and rice. She opened a silk purse and paid for the items with silver chips.

Grey Cloak hooped the rope over his shoulder and loaded the supplies into his arms then followed Zora out the door. "That purse you carry has a familiar jingle to it. Is that my treasure you are spending?"

She gave his pointed ear a tug and said, "You have excellent hearing."

"So it *is* mine. Am I to take it that I am funding this expedition?"

"We all have to make a contribution."

"And now we are going to buy horses with my money?"

As they strolled down the street, she gave him a nod. "You are very perceptive for a young elf."

"Why are we getting horses now? Wouldn't it have made more sense to get them sooner and save time?"

She angled toward a livery stable at the end of town. "Through the Iron Hills?" She gave him a stupefied look. "Horses are goblin meat. They can smell a horse for miles."

"Are you telling me that no one rides a horse through the Iron Hills?"

"Not if they want to keep it," she said.

He shook his head. "I don't believe that. You're only saying what Dalsay and Adanadel say."

"They are wise, and you would be wise to listen to them." Zora stopped at the fence posts that corralled the horses. A black horse with a white patch on his face walked over to her and snorted, and she petted his nose. "This one likes me."

He's not the only one. Grey Cloak petted the horse too. "Like me, he must like beautiful women."

Zora giggled. "This really isn't the time or place for flattery. Besides, I'm not as beautiful as Tatiana is."

"What? Why, of course you are. Sure, she's all elven, like me, and we do have the finest makeup of all the races, but I was taught that it's the inside that counts."

She looked him in the eye and said, "Where did you learn that? Your parents?"

Grey Cloak climbed up on the fence and sat down. "What is Tatiana's story? She's very... well, unique, but what does she do? Is she a wizard like Dalsay?"

"No, she's a healer, among other things. And you changed the subject. Where did you learn that it's what is on the inside that counts? Your parents?"

His jaw tightened.

"Ah," she said. "You don't want to talk about it. I understand."

"What makes you think that you understand? You don't know any more about me than I know about you."

"True, but a blind half elf could see the hurt in your eyes when I asked it. I know that sort of hurt too." She stopped petting the horse and joined him on the fence, sitting hip to hip with him. Watching the sun set, she said, "I'm not an orphan, but I did lose my parents when I was young. I took it upon myself to take care of myself. That's when I met Tanlin. He noticed my resourcefulness. We both saw that in you too. So have you been on your own a long time?"

"I don't want to talk about it." He looked in the corral. "Are you going to buy some horses or sit here and talk?"

With a dejected look, she said, "Buy the horses, I guess."

He hopped off of the fence and headed toward the inn. "Good. Buy them, then."

37

THE COMPANY RODE ON HORSEBACK THROUGH THE harsh terrain of Crow Valley. The bleak land offered little shade from the sun, which burned like a blazing red eye. Instead, the land had gnarled trees and prickly brush. Large insects scurried across the ground and into the cracks. Varmints with bodies padded in fur and spikes chased down the insects, ate them, and vanished into their burrows.

Adanadel and Browning were leading the way. Browning had put on a suit of chain mail, and a coif made of matching chain mail was pulled down around his neck. Dalsay and Tatiana were riding behind them, followed by Tanlin and Zora. Grey Cloak and Dyphestive were bringing up the rear. They had one horse to share, but Grey Cloak walked. No horse could outrun him anyway.

With sweat running down his cheek, Dyphestive said,

"I would be curious to see where we are when we get there."

"Yes, because this place looks like nowhere." Grey Cloak picked up a hunk of dried mud and hurled it at a tall cactus. The mud ball exploded. "I don't even understand how cacti live here."

"It reminds me of Ugrad," Dyphestive said.

Grey Cloak narrowed his eyes and caught up to his brother. He caught the horse by the reins, and through clenched teeth, he said, "Don't utter that again."

"Oh, sorry. It slipped."

"Don't let it slip again." He noticed Zora looking back over her shoulder at them, but he was certain that they were too far away to hear. He hadn't spoken to her since they departed the outskirts of Red Bone, and though he felt bad about it, talk about his parents was a sore spot. He nodded at her and gave a subtle wave. She turned away.

"What's going on between you and her?" Dyphestive asked. "I thought you were getting chummy."

"She pries too much."

"Maybe she wants to know you better."

"Maybe she wants to know you better," Grey Cloak said in a mocking voice. He changed his tone back to normal. "Or maybe she is nosy. Remember, she did steal from us, and she is using *our* chips to fund this expedition."

"Oh." Dyphestive leaned back and looked at the sky. "So now it's *our* chips?"

"I've never said any different. Remember, we are in this for the treasure. I want to get my dagger back from Batram and see what else his arcania has to offer."

"Uh-huh," Dyphestive absentmindedly agreed. His gaze was fixed on Tatiana.

"Stop staring. Zora tells me her gaze can turn a man to stone," Grey Cloak said.

"Really?"

"Do you want to find out?"

"I think."

"You're hopeless."

They traveled down into a large ravine that looked like a huge dried-up riverbed. The winds howled through the shallow canyon. The trek went on for over a league, and the terrain changed. The ground turned into white shale that slipped under foot and hoof and crunched beneath them.

Rounding a bend, they came upon a gargantuan pile of bones. It looked like dragons and great beasts had died in the ravine. Bones from all of the races were scattered all over the ground. They made a pathway of the dead toward a stone tower that stood like a pylon that had dropped from the sky.

Adanadel stopped the company, and he and Dalsay spoke quietly. Then Dalsay dismounted, and with the wind rustling his robes, he headed toward the strange tower.

"Settle yourselves," Adanadel said to the group. "This might take awhile."

While everyone dismounted, Grey Cloak wandered away. He climbed onto a cluster of boulders that gave him a better view of the tower and sat.

The stark tower had two levels. Images were carved in the rock. The bottom level was made of square bright-blue stones that were bigger than men and emanated natural energy. They wrapped around the tower like a ring. The second level had round columns that circled it.

Grey Cloak watched Dalsay approach the building. The tower must have been over one hundred feet tall. He didn't see an entrance, and when Dalsay came within fifty feet of the tower, he vanished. Grey Cloak's arm hairs stood on end. "Zooks."

Tanlin climbed up the rocks and joined Grey Cloak. He was wearing a common set of clothing and a well-worn traveler's cloak, and with his messy hair, he looked like he could blend in anywhere. "Interesting place," he said with a glimmer in his eye.

"It *is* unique. I don't suppose that I'm allowed to know where we are?"

"Don't be silly. This is Dry Bones. Any man or woman in Crow Valley can tell you that." He pointed his slender finger at the tower. "And that's Wizard Watch, or one of them. Gapoli has many."

"Can only wizards enter them?" Grey Cloak asked.

"Hah. You are thinking what I am thinking. I would kill

to see what is inside. A good thief could find his way in, but it's unlikely he would make it out again."

"Sounds like a challenge."

Tanlin nodded. "Indeed."

Grey Cloak pulled his knees to his chest and rolled one thumb over the other, keeping his stare fixed on the tower. He couldn't help but wonder what was in there and was envious that Dalsay was in there and he wasn't. "Aside from the obvious, why is it called Dry Bones? What happened here?"

"There was a war here, long ago, the war of the wizards and the dragons. It wrought such devastation that it nearly wiped out all of Crow Valley. As you can see, the ravages of the war are still visible today. The land was once barren, but it begins to breathe again. Crow Valley was once a land that thrived with milk and honey, the same as our homes back in Westerlund." He took out a pipe made from cattle horn and stuffed some tobacco in the bowl. Scraping a flint stick over the stone, he made a tiny flame, then he lit his pipe and puffed. Smoke rolled out of it.

"Is that it?" He gave Tanlin an incredulous look. "Isn't there more to be said?"

"Oh yeah, there's a lot more to be said." Tanlin huffed out a stream of smoke. "A lot more. But I'm not a historian. Dalsay is."

"Of course you aren't."

38

Tanlin tapped Grey Cloak's shoulder. "No need to pout. I'll fill you in. I only wanted to see how interested you were. A good thief prides himself on the acquisition of knowledge."

"Is that what we are? Thieves?"

"Grave robbers, tomb raiders, treasure snatchers—we go by many names but serve the same purpose. It's not as if we are robbing a good man of his wages. No, we seek what is forgotten. What is lost. What is needed."

"Is that what you called robbing me?"

"No, that was only practice, and you had the smell of a rogue all over you. You stole from them, and we stole from you."

Grey Cloak stiffened. "The gnolls stole from me first!"

"Yes, yes, I know." Tanlin puffed on his pipe. "That's all

in the past. Do you still want to hear about the wizard wars or not?"

"Yes," he said begrudgingly.

"Centuries ago, the dragons and the wizards battled for domination over the races. You see, there was good and evil on both sides. The wizards betrayed one another, and the dragons did the same to themselves." He glanced upward. "That's why you have Sky Riders, good dragons and riders, and Riskers, bad dragons and riders. They say the only reason that good prevailed is because the evil wizards and dragons fought amongst themselves. The moment that happened, the war was lost, or won, rather, for the cause of good, but not before they nearly destroyed half of the world."

Tanlin pointed at the tower. "Shortly after that, the Wizard Watch was created. The wizards vowed to keep the world safe under their watchful gaze. They are supposed to be harbingers of peace. They built the towers in different parts of the world, symbols of protection, but they have been discreet ever since."

"There hasn't been a war since then?"

"Well, not on that scale, not with all of humanity at stake. You see, the wicked dragons took to the north and resided in Dark Mountain. It is there that they breed the Riskers, an army of Dragon Riders that serve the Lord of Dragons, Black Frost. For the longest time, they have been quiet, seemingly banished, but now, a secret war is being waged against the Sky Riders. The Sky Riders are the sworn defenders of Gapoli. They protect the life that is sacred. Black Frost has set his sights on decimating them. With the Sky Riders out of the way, he can wage war against the kingdoms again—and win. He will rule the world he sets up too."

"What about the wizards? Can't they stop them?"

Tanlin left an uncomfortable silence as he gazed at the tower. "I don't even think Dalsay knows where they stand. Apparently, they have a truce of some sort, but a man's word is often broken when a greater temptation intervenes."

"How do you know you can trust Dalsay?"

"I've been with him for over five years. By my standards, he toes the line. So does Adanadel. Both are sworn to serve the greater good of Gapoli."

"Interesting, but I'm more in it for the greater good of Grey Cloak," he joked.

Tanlin chuckled lightly. "We all have our selfish ambitions, but when it comes to Talon, it's important that we all work together. We'll be rewarded for it. If we don't work together, we'll be doomed."

THAT NIGHT, Grey Cloak stood watch over the camp. He'd catnapped earlier and was bright-eyed and bushy-tailed. Something was also gnawing at his stomach. With the others asleep and out of sight, he joined his brother.

"Can't sleep?" Dyphestive asked. He rubbed his eyes and yawned.

"You can sleep if you want. I'll take the rest of the night."

"I'm not going to pass. Are you sure?"

"Yes." He grabbed his brother's arm. "Before you go, I need to tell you something."

"Make it quick, because my bedroll is calling my name." Dyphestive yawned again. "What is it?"

Grey Cloak studied the camp but didn't see anyone else from the company. "I think we should leave."

"What?" Dyphestive asked loudly.

Grey Cloak covered his brother's mouth with his hand. "Will you keep it down?" he whispered harshly. "You heard what I said. What do you think?"

"I think that's crazy. Is this about Zora? Did she hurt your feelings?"

"No, it's not about Zora. It's about something Tanlin said. We were talking, up on the rocks." He pointed at the spot. "He told me about the history of the Wizard Watch. He talked about Dark Mountain, the Riskers, and Black Frost."

Dyphestive paled. "He did? But what does what we are doing have anything to do with that?"

"I don't know, but this isn't the place for us. I think we

should move on. We could work back in Red Bone and settle in that place for a spell."

Dyphestive rubbed one eye and said, "I like where we are now. We can't abandon Talon. That wouldn't be right. We are a part of it now."

Grey Cloak twitched his lips as he thought. "If we get in too deep, we might be running right into what we are running away from."

"And what might that be?" Dalsay asked.

Grey Cloak and Dyphestive spun around.

The wizard had appeared out of nowhere and was staring at them with a harsh expression. His dark eyes bored holes through both of them. "I'm waiting."

39

Dyphestive opened his mouth to speak, but he didn't get a word out before Grey Cloak clamped a hand over his mouth.

"We all have our secrets," Grey Cloak said. He was taking a gamble. It was possible that Dalsay had heard next to nothing. "I don't see how our worries are a concern to you. You won't even tell us where we are going."

"You are an insolent one," Dalsay replied.

"Who? Me? I don't think I'm the only one that falls into that category."

Dalsay's face darkened, and his fingers clenched at his sides. "True. You are both wise and a fool. Go ahead and wrangle with your secret, stripling. I have better things to do. Start packing. We depart immediately." He walked back to the main camp.

The rest of the company crawled out of their tents and began to pack.

"Well done, Grey," Dyphestive said. His eyes followed the wizard. "As if he didn't dislike us enough already, you went and made it worse."

"I don't see how. He doesn't know any more now than he did then."

Dyphestive rolled up his bedroll. "I don't think we are fooling him. I swear I felt his eyes go right through me. Do you think he already knows?"

"No. And quit talking about it." He huffed. "It looks like our opportunity to leave has passed."

"Good," Dyphestive said as he turned his back on his brother and walked away.

"Good to you!"

THE COMPANY ARRIVED at the base of the mountains in Crow Valley the evening of the same day. They were on the west side, which faced the Shelf. Grey Cloak and Dyphestive started to set up camp in the shadows of the jagged mountains, which clawed their way toward the night clouds.

"There won't be any need for that," Dalsay said. The stern mage had been speaking more—to the others, at least— during their trek. "We have arrived where we are meant to be. Now, gather round."

As Adanadel, Tatiana, Browning, Tanlin, and Zora gathered around the wizard, Grey Cloak and Dyphestive wandered away.

"This includes the both of you," Dalsay said.

Excited, Grey Cloak looked at his brother and saw his eyes brighten. They moved in with the group.

"I always keep our purpose secret in case one of us falls into the hands of the enemy," Dalsay said.

Grey Cloak wanted to ask, "What enemy?" but he opted to keep his mouth shut.

Dalsay pushed the sleeves of his robes up, and his hands began to glow with golden fire. "I've scoured the Tomes of Skelar to confirm our destination. A temple that was destroyed during the wizard wars is in these rocks. It's one with the mountain now and full of secrets." A sphere of golden light grew in the palm of his hand, and an image of a temple made in the stone appeared. "We will search for a dragon charm inside the remains of the temple." A sapphire-like gemstone shaped like an eye and shining like a star appeared. "It rests within and is believed to be guarded by demons."

"What sort of demons?" Adanadel asked.

"The possessed undead," Dalsay said. "Among other terrors that I am certain have been manifesting for quite some time in the temple. All of us will go in, but Grey Cloak and Dyphestive, you will remain with the horses and gear. It is imperative that if the need should arise, we make a hasty escape. And there are other wild folk in this land to guard against."

"How long will this take?" Dyphestive asked, and surprise showed on everyone's faces.

"A day or two. No matter what you do, don't leave the horses," Dalsay said. He faced the imposing hills. "Adanadel, take the lead."

The company headed up the slope and vanished into the rocky clefts that awaited them.

"I'll make a fire and get some rice and beans ready," Dyphestive offered.

With his cloak drawn about him, Grey Cloak paced. "It's a test," he muttered.

"What sort of test?" Dyphestive asked as he unloaded his horse, then he fished a small iron frying pan from a sack.

"There isn't a temple in those hills, let alone with a dragon charm in it. It's the silliest thing that I've ever heard." He crossed his arms. "Dalsay is tricking us."

"But he showed us what the temple and charm looked like."

"Yes, another illusion like the one he used at the Red Claw Tavern. Well, he won't be fooling me again." He started picking up rocks and made a ring for the campfire. "I'll be planted right here. Unless we take this opportunity to depart."

Dyphestive sighed. "We can't keep running forever. I

want to see what happens." He poured beans and rice into his pot. "I think this is fun."

"You think backbreaking work is fun. But if they start prying too deep into our business, we are leaving."

"That sounds fair to me."

They made it through the night and spent time during the day keeping the horses fed and in the shade, then nightfall came again.

Grey Cloak flicked a mosquito from his arm. Dyphestive sharpened his sword and hummed a cheerful tune that he'd learned in Havenstock. The night frogs croaked, though no source of water was nearby. Bats dove at insects that littered the night sky.

They were lying on their bedrolls by the fire, hands behind their heads, looking up at the sky.

"Grey, I have a funny feeling in my gut," Dyphestive stated. "Do you think the others are all right?"

"Of course they are. I bet they are watching us from a perch on the hills and laughing."

"True, but they don't have any supplies. Wouldn't they get hungry? Thirsty?"

"No doubt *you* would, but they probably don't have stomachs half as big as yours." He sniggered. "It takes less to fill them. Go ahead and get some sleep. I'll stand watch. I can't sleep through this, anyway."

"Fine by me. Good night." Dyphestive closed his eyes.

Within seconds, he was breathing softly though his nose. His sword was lying beside his chest.

The wind picked up and whistled through the mountains. Grey Cloak paced the camp with his arms behind his back. He wanted adventure and treasure. Instead, he was doing nothing more than being a common hireling for another selfish group of people.

This is a game. Another one of Dalsay's games. Either that or they are going to keep the treasure for themselves.

He caught movement out of the corner of his eye. *What is that?*

Instead of freezing and sounding the alarm, he went about his business. Someone was huddled against the rocks. He noticed them shift in the dimness of the night. *I bet it's Zora or Tanlin. They are testing me.*

He moved out of the person's line of sight and stole into the hills then crept over the rocks until he was over the person spying on him. Huddled in the shadows, the person was lying in wait. In the dark, it was hard to make out their shape.

I'm no fool. I know it's you, Tanlin or Zora. He pounced on the person's back. "Aha!"

The figure grabbed Grey Cloak's arm and flipped him over his shoulder. Then he pounced on Grey Cloak and started to pummel him. *You're not Tanlin or Zora!*

40

GREY CLOAK TWISTED OUT FROM UNDERNEATH HIS attacker and put him in a headlock, holding tight. "Who are you?" His nose crinkled. "You smell."

The attacker stood all the way up, lifting Grey Cloak off his feet, then charged backward and rammed him into a boulder.

"Oof!" Grey Cloak lost his grip.

His assailant skirted free of his grasp. The man's clothing was in shambles, and his hair was long and stringy.

As they circled each other, the clouds cleared and cast moonlight on the man's face.

"You!"

It was the hermit they'd encountered in the gnoll's dungeon. He pointed his scaly fingers back at Grey Cloak and said, "You!"

They danced in a circle, feinting left and right. The hermit was much bigger than Grey Cloak remembered. Before, he'd been crammed in a cell, but now he was full height though hunched over. He moved with catlike quickness too.

Dyphestive came barreling out of nowhere. He dove at the hermit, who jumped out of the way only to have Grey Cloak tackle his legs.

"I've got him! I've got him!" Grey Cloak said. "I'm not sure *why* I have him. He smells like cattle."

Grabbing him by the hair, the hermit pulled back and said in a crazy voice, "Let go of me, little elf! I'll feed you to my flock!"

Dyphestive piled on top of them then locked his arms around the hermit and slammed him down. Somehow, the hermit twisted his way out of his mighty grip and bounded away like a deer.

They chased the hermit all over the camp. His wild hair streamed behind his back. Grey Cloak caught him and tripped him, and Dyphestive jumped on his back.

The hermit wormed his way free time after time, and finally, he stopped, dropped to a knee, and panted. "Stop. I surrender."

They exchanged dumbfounded looks.

Grey Cloak said, "You attacked us."

"No, you jumped on my back and attacked me. You win."

"What do you want, hermit? And how did you get here?"

The hermit cleared his throat, slowly came to his feet, and said, "I came to warn you. Your friends are in danger. Those black hills have taken them."

Grey Cloak fanned his cloak, knocking the dust off. "We know that."

"No! You don't know anything. You must save your friends. Save them soon, or they will all be dead."

"How do you know this?"

"I have visions." The hermit stared up at the starry expanse. "I see with my eyes wide open. I can see yesterday, today, and tomorrow at times. You must go. You must steal the dragon."

"You mean dragon charm," Dyphestive said.

"Don't tell this vagrant that." Grey Cloak shooed the hermit away with his hands. "Go. Go away."

"Maybe we should feed him," Dyphestive suggested.

"If we feed him, he'll never leave."

"Mmm, I could use a hot meal." The hermit rubbed a circle on his tummy and licked his lips. "What's cooking?"

"Nothing."

"Beans and rice," Dyphestive said.

The hermit kicked his heels up as he sauntered over to the campfire, then he grabbed a spoon and helped himself. "Beans and rice. Yum, yum, yum. I like beans and rice. Beans and rice are fun."

"Do you have a name, hermit?" Dyphestive asked as he offered the man a waterskin.

"Will you quit feeding him? We don't know where he has been," Grey Cloak said.

"I am *hungry*."

"No, a real name," Dyphestive said.

"Call me what you want. It doesn't matter. I have many names. Some far too long to say." The hermit licked the spoon clean. "Long, long, long—a river is long, but not all rivers are deep, deep, deep. Don't forget some rivers leave dust on your feet."

Grey Cloak pulled his brother aside. "When Dalsay returns, you will have a lot of explaining to do."

Dyphestive shrugged. "He seems harmless and friendly."

"This is the same man that called the gnolls down on our heads when we tried to free him. And can you explain to me how he was able to follow us? That's no ordinary hermit."

"What is he? A special hermit?"

"A trickster. Pixie, fairy, or enchanter. If we lose the horses, that's on your head." Grey Cloak threw his arms up. "Oh, why do I even care?"

"It's good that you do." Dyphestive's eyes enlarged, and he tapped Grey Cloak on the shoulder and pointed toward the hills.

A woman was staggering down from the mountain

path. Her cloak was in tatters, and a hollow look hung in her eyes.

Grey Cloak ran to her. "Zora!"

41

ZORA COLLAPSED IN GREY CLOAK'S ARMS. HE CARRIED her over to the campfire.

"She's so cold."

Her eyes were sunken in and milky white. Her pale, clammy skin showed blue veins rising in her face, and she had gashes through her clothing.

He gently shook her. "Zora. Zora. Talk to me!"

Dyphestive kneeled beside them and took her hand in his. "She's ice cold. What happened to her?"

The hermit hobbled over and looked down on the young half-elf woman. "Pretty thing. She's been stricken by demons. Fatal. Time is precious, or she will turn."

"What do you mean, 'turn'?" Grey Cloak asked as he removed his cloak and covered her body. Her breath came out in visible chilly vapor.

"She'll live as the dead. Time is precious. You must go." The hermit shoved Dyphestive. "I told you there was danger. Yet you waste time. Go!" He pushed Grey Cloak. "Go! Your companions need you."

"This better not be one of Dalsay's tricks." Grey Cloak removed Zora's belt of daggers and buckled it to his waist.

Dyphestive grabbed his iron sword. Then he took a torch from one of the horses and lit it in the campfire.

"You better not harm her, hermit," Grey Cloak warned.

"The harm has already been done. Stop flapping your tongue. I'll keep her safe." The hermit scooted her closer to the fire. "Don't hesitate. Swing. Give them a taste of your iron."

Grey Cloak led the way up into the mountain. His keen eyes found Zora's shuffling impressions on the ground. Her staggered path snaked its way through the low-hanging branches of the trees. His heart raced.

Night birds and varmints darted through the branches. The night owls made spooky hoots. A wild beast howled. They followed the trail hundreds of yards until they came upon a large fallen pillar of stone. Ancient rubble was scattered and broken all over the woodland.

Grey Cloak jumped onto the six-foot-thick pillar and faced a temple that looked like it had been smashed in by a giant rock. Tons of debris half blocked the only visible entrance.

Dyphestive started to climb onto the pillar. With a sword in one hand and a torch in the other, he struggled.

"Give me that," Grey Cloak said as he took the torch.

Dyphestive climbed up and over the pillar, and they headed toward the entrance.

A ghoul burst out of a nest of debris covered in overgrowth. He lunged at Dyphestive, whose instincts made him spring into action. He swung sideways, and the iron sword sheared the ghoulish man in two. The top half of his body fell to the left, and the legs collapsed to the right.

Dyphestive's nostrils flared. He looked down on the undead and said, "Don't forget to swing."

Grey Cloak held the torch over the creature. It had been a man once but had turned into an abomination of rotting flesh and bone. "Well done, brother." He pulled out one of Zora's daggers and ventured toward the entrance again. "Well done."

The inside of the temple was pitch black. An unnatural cold swept through their clothing, carrying the stale stench of death.

"We always wanted to see what Gapoli had to offer. We can check off another spot by going in here." Grey Cloak walked into the dimness. His torch cast light on an atrium filled with dead plant life. Petrified trees stretched toward a broken skylight. "Walk quietly. Perhaps what thrives here won't expect us."

Dyphestive nodded, and they moved deeper into the

temple, across the point where it connected with the mountain. The vines and overgrowth that filled the temple entrance merged with cut block and natural stone and began to thin. Faces of people from all of the races were carved into the walls. A fountain, long dried up and wrapped in vines, was positioned in the middle of two staircases that led down.

Grey Cloak crouched at the top of the right staircase and bent his ear toward the steps. He heard faint scuffling echoing through the deep chambers and pointed downward.

Dyphestive leaned over the left staircase and narrowed his eyes. The sound of footsteps slapping on stone raced up the stairs, and he thrust his sword downward.

Grey Cloak jumped to his aid. A ghoul was lanced on Dyphestive's blade. Its gnarled hands clawed at him, and it began to push its undead body along the sword.

Dyphestive gave the handle of his sword a fierce twist. The violent move bored a hole in the ghoul's shambling body. Its arms trembled, and the glow in its white eyes went dim. With a heave of his shoulders, Dyphestive slung the ghoul off the sword and into the wall. It tumbled down the steps.

Grey Cloak put his hand on his brother's shoulder and said, "Whatever you do, don't let those things touch you. Those claws match the marks on Zora."

Without warning, black tendrils snaked their way

across the floor from the right stairwell and slipped around Grey Cloak's ankles. He looked down and said, "Huh?"

The black tendrils yanked Grey Cloak off his feet. He dropped the torch and stabbed at the snakelike roots.

Dyphestive lunged for his brother, but the vines growing around the fountain were quicker. They entangled his arms and legs in a moment.

Grey cloak stabbed the tendrils, but they did not give. They hauled him toward the stairs. His free hand's fingers clawed at the ground, searching for purchase. He fastened his grip on a lip of the stone flooring and hung on for dear life. With a fierce tug, the tendrils ripped him down the stairs and into the suffocating well of darkness.

42

"Grey!" Dyphestive strained against the vines binding him. The muscles in his brawny arms heaved and flexed, but the vines had entwined themselves around him from the ankle to the thigh and the wrist to the elbow, squeezing.

He dropped his sword, and the metal rang when it hit the ground. When he tried to march forward toward the torch on the floor, the vines yanked him backward toward the fountain. Inside the fountain, a spring of oily black water churned with sinister life. The vines were tugging him toward the ghastly bath.

"No," he said. "Nooo!" Dyphestive managed to brace his foot against the rim of the fountain, and he pushed off with all of his strength. The smaller vines snapped and gave way, but the thicker vines tightened on his limbs.

"No plant is going to beat me," he huffed. "No plant will stop me. I will save my brother."

A smaller vine slid up his back and coiled around his mouth. "Ulp!"

Maddened like a trapped bull, Dyphestive thrust his full weight against the entanglement. He found enough purchase on the ground and dove forward, and he was able to wrap his straining fingers around the shaft of the torch. Then he jammed the flames on the vines.

But the fire harmlessly danced on the vines, and they hauled him back to the fountain, which was filling with burbling black ooze.

Dyphestive thrashed against his living bindings. Another vine coiled around the thick muscles in his neck, and he choked. It hauled him even closer to the hungry dark waters of the fountain.

With his face as red as a beet, Dyphestive turned toward the fountain and thrust the fiery torch into the oily waters. The wild *skreeel* of nature and magic torn asunder erupted from the fountain as its dark waters burst into flame.

Dyphestive ripped free of his flaming restraints and tumbled to the ground. The fountain's water jumped and roared with flame. A ghostly spirit fled from it and diminished with one final howl.

In a cold sweat, with his fingers locked on his torch,

Dyphestive picked up his sword and headed downstairs after Grey Cloak.

GREY CLOAK WAS DRAGGED down the steps like a sack of onions into the underbelly of the temple. The creature dragging him left a coat of slime behind it. The bulky black thing scurried down the twisting hallways on many tiny legs. *What is this thing?*

The more Grey Cloak kicked, the more futile his situation became. The monster's tendrils only bit deeper into his ankles with crushing pain. He let his body slacken and slid another dagger out of his sheath. *Let's see where this thing takes me.*

His keen vision started to adjust to the darkness, and he could make out the outlines of the walls and chambers he passed. There was no sign of the others.

The creature dragged him into a chamber that was littered with old barrels and wooden crates and stopped against the wall. Grey Cloak got his first good look at the monster. It was a shapeless bulk of wobbly flesh over four feet in height and hundreds of pounds. It was faceless, aside from a large mouth filled with tiny rows of teeth. Many long tentacles wriggled around its body like wild hair. Its fetid breath reeked of death, and its jaw opened and closed with loud chomping snaps.

"Perhaps this will be more to your liking," Grey Cloak said as he hooked his fingers on a small barrel and hurled it into the monster's mouth.

The creeper chewed the barrel to bits, the wood splintering in its mouth, and reeled Grey Cloak in more quickly. His head hit the floor as he slipped across the stone.

The monster's mouth opened and closed. Deep inside its gullet, something like a heart pulsated. *What's this?*

He braced his boots against the creature's slime-covered bottom lip and timed the hungry jaws quickly closing up and down. Eyeing the glimmering pulsation within, he muttered, "Here goes everything," then he thrust his entire arm and shoulder into the mouth of the creeper.

The dagger tip bit deep into something, and the creeper shuddered. Its great jaws locked open, and the tendrils fell away from Grey Cloak's ankles.

He crawled away, panting. "Phew, that was close."

Once he caught his breath, he dusted his grimy clothes off and said, "And these were new." He rubbed the fabric of his sleeve. "Well made. Nothing is torn."

He turned toward the chamber's exit, but two ghouls were blocking his path, and they advanced on him. Grey Cloak cocked his arms back and threw both of his daggers at the same time.

The blades sank deep into the middle of each ghoul's forehead. Their advance slowed, and they aimlessly shuffled through the room. He slipped between them, pulled two more daggers from his belt, and exited the chamber. Then he quickly ducked into a crouch.

Swish! A sword blade bit into the stone archway just above his head. "Dyphestive, what are you doing? Trying to kill me?"

"Sorry. I saw those demons going in," Dyphestive said apologetically as he yanked his sword free. "Are you hurt?"

"Thankfully, I still have my *head* attached to my shoulders. And they are ghouls, not demons. I think Dalsay exaggerates. Where were you?"

"I got attacked by a plant."

"Did it hurt?"

"Sort of."

"Good. Come on. We have to find the others and save Zora." At a brisk pace, he made his way down the corridor.

The bodies of ghouls were piled on the floor. They were all dead from sword cuts and magic that scorched skin and bone. The destroyed flesh left a strong lingering stink. Grey Cloak and Dyphestive stepped over the wreckage of undead flesh and moved onward.

The corridor spilled into an open worship chamber that had been hewn from a natural cavern. Stalactites and stalagmites accompanied tall columns that were barely holding up the jagged, dripping ceiling. Lit torches lined the exterior walls.

More ghouls lay strewn across the floor. They were in worse shape than the others. It looked like a hurricane had torn through them. Standing among the heaps of ghouls were the members of Talon, their faces mortified and grim, their bodies frozen in space and time.

An unnatural chill wind swirled throughout the chamber, and Grey Cloak's veins turned to ice.

"It's so cold," Dyphestive said. "What is happening?"

43

Grey Cloak inspected the bodies of his rigid friends. They were all covered in frost. Dalsay's robes were stiff, and his fingers were clutching at the air. His eyes didn't move. Adanadel and Browning's swords were cocked back to swing. Tanlin was crouched, brandishing a short sword. Tatiana was clutching a golden amulet with an orange gemstone in the center.

"Do you think they are dead?" Dyphestive asked as he put a finger on Browning's face. He snapped his fingers, but nothing happened.

"They are catatonic, but the question is how?" Grey Cloak swept his gaze through the chamber.

At the back end of the chamber, a long row of stone steps led up to a statue of a godlike being. She was a beautiful woman dressed in vines and leaves. A dragon tail curled around her legs. The nose was broken off of her otherwise-perfect face. Also in the room were more tunnel entrances that led deeper into the caves.

Grey Cloak's mind raced. Whoever the company was fighting had disappeared. *Where did they go?*

"Should we carry them out of here?" Dyphestive asked.

Grey Cloak stroked his chin. "I don't know." His skin was crawling. Something wasn't right. "Keep an eye out. There have to be more ghouls around here, or something else."

Dyphestive prowled the area with his two-handed sword ready. He poked it into the ghouls lying on the floor. One of them twitched and clawed at him harmlessly.

Grey Cloak studied Tatiana. The elven mystic's eyes were set with determination. Fire lurked within but was trapped inside. The amulet she was carrying twinkled as it caught the flickering torchlight. He started to touch her cheek but pulled back at the sound of a haunting voice.

"I wouldn't do that if I were you." The strange voice was dark and sinister. "Your touch will spell your doom."

They moved back to back with their heads on a swivel but saw no source for the voice.

"But you may join your companions. Your doom was sealed the moment you entered. Now, you will feed my brethren. My ghouls. *My pet.*"

Something scurried across the floor in the dark. A tail flickered into view then vanished between the stalagmites.

"There." Grey Cloak pointed and moved toward the creature, peeking around the stalagmites. Something was huddled against the damp rocks. Its eyes were shards of shiny ice, and it was the size of a small dog and had scales all over it. "Dragon," he said and swallowed the lump in his throat.

"Did you say, 'dragon'?" Dyphestive asked.

"Aye, a bit of a small one," he replied. The dragon's scales were white and dull silver, rough, and it had spiny ridges on its back. Grey Cloak couldn't tear his eyes away from its gaze. His limbs froze, and the word caught in his throat when he tried to say, "Dyphestive."

"Ghouls," Dyphestive warned. He bumped against his brother. "Why aren't you moving? Ghouls are coming."

Out of the corner of his mouth, he managed to say, "I can't."

Head low, the small cave dragon slunk forward.

FOUR GHOULS CREPT out of the corners. Shoulders low and arms hanging, they moved in toward Dyphestive. They had once been men, but their bodies had become gnarled, and their long, sharp fingernails clicked together like some sort of animal sound.

Dyphestive charged the fastest-moving ghoul and brought his sword down in a long arcing chop. *Slice!* The blow hewed the ghoul through the shoulder. He pulled the sword out in time to launch a second swing and cut the legs out from underneath the nearest advancing ghoul. It flopped on the stones, wiggled, and hissed.

Just as Dyphestive turned toward his final two aggressors, one of them plowed into his back. He tripped over a ghoul corpse and smacked his head against a hunk of fallen stone. Stars burst in his eyes.

The ghouls piled on Dyphestive, and their sharp fingernails and teeth tore at his body. All he could think was *I should have worn armor*.

THE CAVE DRAGON stared at Grey Cloak, who couldn't move a muscle. The dragon came nose to nose with him and licked his face with its icy tongue. *You scaly varmint. Quit licking me!*

The dragon climbed on Grey Cloak's back and fastened its claws into his skin. *Ow!* Its tail coiled around his neck, and it rested its head over his shoulder. *Now you're just being weird. What? Wait, what are you doing?*

Its tail pulsed with power, and its mind flowed into the body of Grey Cloak. Without even thinking it, he stood, not under his own power but by the command of the dragon. His body was not his own—it was the dragon's.

He had a full view of the entire room. Dyphestive was

battling for his life in a knot of thrashing limbs, the ghouls tearing at his body. Blood ran down the side of his face. The members of Talon stood as rigid as statues, with more frost caking over them.

The haunting voice spoke again. It wasn't the cave dragon speaking, as Grey Cloak first thought, but someone else entirely. "Ah, I see that you found my pet, elf. You will make an excellent meal." An apparition of a woman glided through the dragon goddess statue and hovered over the room.

The apparition was wearing ceremonial burial robes. Underneath the hood, her face shifted between beautiful and ghastly. The ghost pointed a bony finger at Grey Cloak. "My pet likes you." She pointed at Dyphestive. "And my ghouls like you." She gave a chilling cackle. "Welcome to my undead army."

44

THE GHOST DRIFTED CLOSER TO GREY CLOAK AND hovered before him. She spoke in a haunting voice. "So many have come to find my glory, but all have failed. Now, they join my army. It grows stronger with the passage of time. Soon, all of Crow Valley will be mine again."

Grey Cloak pulled at the long dragon tail locked around his throat. It was tighter than iron, but he could still talk. "It appears that your army is dwindling."

"I am Bella Shon May, high priestess of this temple. All of Crow Valley shall be mine," she said.

"Yes, you mentioned that, Bella." He dropped to his knee. Out of the corner of his eye, he could see Dyphestive still thrashing against the ghouls. "I can't help but wonder how such a pretty priestess lives in a dark place such as this."

"My temple is the greatest in all of the realm. My worshippers flock to see me. I am their night. My stars are their light. I am the queen of Crow Valley."

"It is clear that you are all-powerful and invincible. Only a goddess such as you could control a dragon such as this." He groaned and lowered his other knee as the small dragon's claws tightened in his back. "Ugh!"

"I am immortal. None can stop the likes of me." Her body floated among the members of Talon. "They could not defeat what they did not see. When their eyes opened, it was too late. They came to serve themselves, but now they only serve me. Forever."

DYPHESTIVE LOCKED a ghoul's arm in his, and he head-butted it in the nose. The ghouls were strong, but he was stronger. He flipped one ghoul into the other and tackled them both. They wrestled over the floor like ravenous wildcats. The ghouls' fingernails burned like fire as they slashed against his skin.

Sluggishness worked its way into Dyphestive's blood, but he locked his arms around one ghoul's neck and squeezed until bone cracked. The last ghoul latched onto Dyphestive's back and bit down hard on his neck. He reached back, grabbed a handful of tangled hair, and ripped it out. Then he charged backward into the stalagmites and smashed the ghoul between them. The ghoul's grip loosened.

Dyphestive twisted around, picked up the ghoul and raised it over his head then slammed it down on a sharp stalagmite. On wobbly legs, he spun around. His fingertips were tingling and starting to turn numb. Black veins rose in his arms.

His iron sword was lying on the ground, and he stumbled toward it and fell. Limbs stiffening, he forced himself up to his hands and knees. He could see Grey Cloak talking to a ghost, and a dragon was latched to his back. The ghost's hands stretched toward Grey Cloak's face.

Dyphestive screamed, "Nooo!"

"DON'T you think your grand intentions would be better served if I remained alive, in the flesh?" Grey Cloak asked. *Buy time. Buy time. Buy time.* "I could lead many more followers directly to you. Why, we could increase your army tenfold in a month."

Bella clawed her fingers in front of his face. "My touch is all I need." She cackled. "See the ones that sought me." She pointed at the paralyzed party. "They are mine, mine, mine. Yes, you too, elf, with marrow as sweet as a honeycomb."

"Are you certain that this is what you want? Another

catatonic follower? Why, can any of these ghouls sing your praises? I have an excellent singing voice," he said. "If I could only clear my throat."

"Silence!" Her voice shook the water drops off of the tips of the stalactites.

Her word seized Grey Cloak's tongue, and he lost control of his body again. He didn't know how, but she controlled the dragon, and the dragon controlled him. His efforts to persuade her had failed.

Bella poked a finger at his nose. "Crow Valley will be mine. The lilies of the fields will be mine. The robins in the trees will be mine. The dwarves in the valleys will be mine. You, elf, will be mine. All of you are mine." Her face shifted from beautiful to skeletal to beautiful and back to skeletal. "Now, for a kiss that will last you forever."

Grey Cloak's will battled back against the unseen powers that were harnessing his body. *Never!* He jerked to one side.

Bella's lips connected with the face of the dragon, which spat icy breath through her ghostly body and jumped to the floor then scurried into the stalagmites and vanished.

"Nooo!" Bella glared at Grey Cloak. "You trickster. You shall die!" She swiped at him.

Grey Cloak did a back handspring away from her skeletal fingers then snaked out two daggers and hurled them at her. The blades passed right through her body.

"Fool! You cannot harm me. I am immortal!" She drew

up like a sheet full of wind, and wind roared around her body. "Die, mortal. Die!"

"You first," Grey Cloak said as he reached for two more daggers. But his scabbard was empty. "Or maybe not." He backed toward the wall, searching for a weapon.

Dyphestive lumbered between the ghost and Grey Cloak with his sword in hand and moved with rigid limbs. His face turned white, and black veins filled it, just like Zora's. "Stay back or die!" he said in a dry voice.

Bella Shon May let out a victorious bone-chilling laugh and attacked.

45

Dᴙᴘʜᴇꜱᴛɪᴠᴇ ʟᴜɴɢᴇᴅ ᴀᴛ ᴛʜᴇ ɢʜᴏꜱᴛ. Hɪꜱ ᴛᴡᴏ-ʜᴀɴᴅᴇᴅ sword stabbed through the misty vapors of Bella Von May's body like flesh and bone.

The ghost let out an ear-splitting shriek. "Nooo! Nooo! Nooo!" she howled. The apparition's body began to flex and crinkle. "The iron burns! The iron burns!" She started to dissipate like ash in a fire. "The iron burrrnnsss..." Bella Von May's body burst apart, drifted away like snowflakes, and disappeared in the air.

The iron sword fell from Dyphestive's grip, and Grey Cloak ran to his swaying brother's aid. He held him up by putting his arm around his waist and pulling Dyphestive's arm over his shoulder then walked him forward. "Stay with me. Stay with me."

Dyphestive gave a ragged sigh. "What's wrong with me?"

"I don't think we have time to go into all of that."

The members of Talon's bodies came back to life, and they staggered on their feet and shook their heads.

Tatiana's wide-eyed stare landed on Dyphestive, and the beautiful elven mystic rushed over to them. "Lay him down," she ordered.

Dyphestive had dark gashes and bruises all over his body, and his skin was pasty white.

"This is my fault," Tatiana said with a grieved look on her face. "I should have sensed the ghost. She took me by surprise." She clasped Dyphestive's hand, sharing her amulet's power with him."

"Zora," Dyphestive groaned. "Save Zora."

Tatiana squeezed her eyes shut and said, "Be silent." She started muttering arcane words at a feverish pace, and the amulet glowed with radiant fire. The light spread up Dyphestive's arm and through his body.

Grey Cloak's eyes widened as he felt the warmth from the light.

The black veins in Dyphestive's arms and face subsided, and his color returned. He smiled at Tatiana. "Will you marry me?"

"I'm certain you cured him," Grey Cloak said to her.

"Yes." With a warm smile, she caressed Dyphestive's face and gave him an inquisitive look. "He heals fast."

"We have to go save Zora," Grey Cloak said.

"I'm here," Zora said. She'd come through the front entrance of the worship chamber. Her skin had returned to normal.

Grey Cloak ran to her and said, "How? Not that I'm complaining, but you were the walking dead."

"The hermit cured me."

"He did?"

She shrugged. "I didn't imagine it. But you can ask him yourself. He is with the horses. He said, 'Return. It's safe. They'll be waiting for you.'"

Dalsay picked up Dyphestive's sword and stared at the iron blade. "Fate favors us today. Who'd have known that the apparition had such a simple weakness." He reached down and helped Dyphestive to his feet. "You did well, stripling." He turned to Grey Cloak. "Both of you." Giving Dyphestive back his sword, he continued, "Who would have thought a worthless piece of iron could save us."

Tanlin hugged Zora.

Browning shook Grey Cloak and Dyphestive's hands. He made a clicking sound out of the side of his mouth and said, "I don't ever want to be that cold again." He brushed the frost off his chain mail. "Ever. Dalsay, let's find that treasure. I want my share. It's time to retire."

"You always say that," Tanlin said.

"Well, this time it's true," Browning fired back.

"Dalsay," Tatiana said, "this is all my error. I apologize. My oversight could have killed us all."

The wizard lifted a brow and said, "Yes, that is exactly what I was thinking the entire time my innards were freezing and I saw the gates of the Realm of Death coming toward me."

Tatiana's shoulders slumped, and her chin fell.

Dalsay gently put a hand on her face. "We all share in failure and victory as well. Onward." He kissed her on the forehead. "Now let's find that treasure."

Grey Cloak looked at them curiously. *Odd. Are Dalsay and Tatiana together?* He nudged Zora.

"Don't ask," she said.

Dalsay moved up the stairs to the dragon lady's statue's feet. A stone sarcophagus was in front of it. "Bella Von May was laid to rest here. She was part of a race that worshipped dragons. Her people emulated them." As everyone gathered around him, he placed his hand on the oversized sarcophagus's lid. "Stand back."

The air in the cavern shimmered, and the ring finger on Dalsay's right hand glowed. The stone lid cracked loudly and broke into several sections. With strain in his voice, he said, "Remove the stones."

They all grabbed one stone at a time. The puzzle pieces of rock hovered magically in the air. Every piece was tossed aside.

"Good," Dalsay said. The fire in his ring went out.

They surrounded the tomb and peered inside. It was empty.

"May I?" Tanlin asked Dalsay.

Dalsay nodded.

Tanlin climbed into the large coffin and began knocking on the floor. He scooted his feet over the surface. "It's as hard as rock. Nothing underneath."

Dalsay stroked the corners of his mouth and said, "True riches lie at her feet." He walked around the twelve-foot-high statue.

Grey Cloak followed his path and said, "Let's not forget there is still a dragon on the loose."

"I'm very aware. More so than you are," Dalsay said. "Everyone, keep looking and be wary of the dragon. More ghouls could be among us too." He moved back to the front sarcophagus, leaned against it, and closed his eyes. "I must concentrate."

The company meandered through the cavern.

Grey Cloak caught up with Dyphestive, who was wandering between the columns. "Are you certain you are well?"

"I've never felt better. But I could use something to eat."

"Of course you could." He eyed the statue's feet. "Listen, I have a notion."

"A what?"

"A thought. An idea. Do you think you can push that statue over?"

Dyphestive's brow creased, but he said, "Yes."

"Do it." He led his brother up the steps.

Dyphestive set his hands against the dragon tail of the statue and started to push. "Hurk!"

But the statue didn't budge.

46

"Put your legs into it!" Grey Cloak said.

"Sorry. Sometimes I forget, but I'm getting better." Dyphestive squatted down and heaved against the statue. It began to teeter, and stone scraped over stone.

Browning hustled up the stairs and put his weight against it. "Let's make some noise!"

The statue fell over on its side, and the stone broke into several large pieces.

Dalsay rushed up to the landing. "What have you done? Are you trying to wake the rest of the dead?"

A square chamber the size of a small bath was underneath the statue's feet. It was filled with treasure.

Grey Cloak's smile grew large. With gold and rubies shining in his eyes, he jumped into the pile and sprinkled his body with the jingling coins.

With his big fists on his broad hips, Browning leaned over the trove and said, "Now that's a haul."

Dalsay pulled Grey Cloak out of the pile by his hair. "You try my patience, stripling. I don't find your antics amusing." He shoved Grey Cloak toward Dyphestive. "Stay put!"

Grey Cloak crossed his arms over his chest and said, "Well, that's gratitude for you."

Adanadel stepped in front of Grey Cloak and said, "You would be wise to keep your thoughts to yourself." Then he turned his attention back to Dalsay.

Dalsay stepped into the trove and began shoveling coins aside. "There are treasures worth more than silver and gold. The dragon charm is what we seek."

Tanlin bent over the pool of coins and gemstones. He had a sack in his hand. Dalsay scooped up handfuls of coins and poured them into the bags.

"I've never even imagined so much money before," Dyphestive said.

"You must not have a very big imagination," Grey Cloak said, but his mouth was watering.

Zora cozied up between them. "You are right. There are treasure troves such as this that can fill the very floor of this cavern. The problem is it's not possible to carry it all out."

"I would find a way," Grey Cloak said.

"Dalsay," Adanadel said in a warning tone.

The mage looked up, and Adanadel pointed at a nearby

stalagmite. The cave dragon was perched on top of it, its piercing eyes fixed on Dalsay. Adanadel pulled his sword, and the rest of the company fanned out in front of the dragon and readied their weapons.

"Everyone remain still," Dalsay said. His hands were submerged in the coins. "I suspect that the ghost of Bella Von May controlled the dragon by tapping into the dragon charm. Now, the creature is free to do as it wishes. And it wishes to have this treasure."

The dragon's tongue flicked out of its mouth as it bared its sharp teeth.

"Should we kill it?" Browning said.

"And risk one of us dying?" Dalsay asked. "No. That cave dragon might be small, but it's not young. Look at its scales—full-grown and strong." He pulled his hand free and gazed at the object in his palm. A blue sapphire the size of an egg and shaped like an eye burned brightly. He lifted it up for all to see. "The dragon charm. I have it."

The dragon's eyes shone the same radiant blue as the sapphire, and it crawled down the stalagmite to the floor.

"Everyone, back away slowly," Dalsay ordered. New sweat built up on his brow. "We are leaving."

"What? Without the treasure?" Grey Cloak objected.

"Do as I say!" Dalsay said.

Head low, the cave dragon slunk forward, and Zora, Tatiana, and Browning backed away from the trove as Dalsay climbed up with Tanlin by his side.

Grey Cloak walked closer to the trove. It had thousands of coins with small gems sprinkled among them. He bent over to scoop more coins out.

Browning grabbed him by the cloak and pulled him away. "Don't be a fool."

"You have a dragon charm. Use it on the dragon, Dalsay."

"I am. It's the only reason the dragon hasn't attacked yet." Sweat dripped off of the tip of his hawkish nose. "Can you not see? This dragon is not alone."

Grey Cloak's gaze swept through the cavern. Something moved in the stalactites, and two more cave dragons crawled down from the jagged rocks. One of the dragons dropped to the floor beside its brother. The third one dropped as well, creating a trio. Their long tails curled up behind their backs like scorpions' tails. As one, they crept forward.

Dyphestive hooked Grey Cloak's arm. "Come on." They backed away and joined the others.

Grey Cloak took one last look at all of the treasure they were leaving behind. It left him with one thought in mind. *I hate Dalsay.*

Without words, the company departed the temple and headed down the hill. The horses and gear were waiting for them at the bottom, but there was no sign of the hermit. Dalsay had a scowl on his face, and Grey Cloak was fuming.

"Ready the horses for travel," Dalsay said to Dyphestive and Grey Cloak.

The mage pulled the other members of the company together and left them to themselves. The members of Talon listened to Dalsay and Browning's heated exchange.

Dyphestive was holding his horse's reins, and he petted its nose. "It doesn't sound good."

"Yes, you would think they would be happy that they aren't dead. We saved them. They should be thanking us," Grey Cloak said. "And what sort of treasure hunters leave so much treasure?" He gazed at the mountains. "I say we go back. What are dragons going to do with those chips? Spend them?"

Dyphestive managed a dry chuckle. "I think we are lucky to be alive."

"You are starting to sound like the others."

Tanlin and Zora approached. They had grim looks on their faces.

"We want you to know that we appreciate the bravery you showed in the temple," Tanlin said.

"Yes, we are grateful," Zora added.

"But..." Grey Cloak said.

Tanlin handed each of them a small purse filled with jingling coins. "This is your share from the sack I stole from the temple. You more than earned it. *But* the members of Talon voted. We've decided to part ways with you from here on out."

He and Zora turned away.

Zora had a sad look on her face when she turned and said, "And you can keep the horse."

47

THE MEMBERS OF TALON RODE OFF, LEAVING A CLOUD of dust behind them, and Dyphestive felt a sense of dread in the pit of his stomach. He poured the sack of chips into his hand. There were at least a couple dozen silver coins and a few gold.

"That's nothing compared to what awaits us back in the temple," Grey Cloak said with a twinkle in his eye.

"This is more than I've ever had." Dyphestive gave Grey Cloak an incredulous look. "More than we have ever had."

"Not true—we had more when I stole from those gnolls." Grey Cloak tossed his purse by the campfire and pointed at the company, which was vanishing in the distance. "That they stole from us."

"I liked them."

"You liked Dalsay? Really?"

"I didn't bull up on him like you did."

"No, of course not. You don't question anything. You are happy to go along wherever the wind blows."

Dyphestive stood over his brother and overshadowed him. "That's not so. I'm questioning you. You and your hardheaded stupidity." He pushed Grey Cloak.

"Have you lost your mind? I will throttle you."

"Is that so?" He pushed Grey Cloak again. "I would like to see that."

"What are you going to do? Hit me with your anvil? I don't think so. And you call *me* stupid. You are the one that keeps an anvil for a pet."

Dyphestive rushed Grey Cloak.

But Grey Cloak easily slipped away from his clutching fingers. "Don't make a fool of yourself. Trying to catch me will leave the horse laughing."

"When I get ahold of you, I'm going to teach you a lesson you'll never forget." He chased his brother over the dusty terrain. He wasn't slow by any means and was quick by most men's standards, but catching Grey Cloak was like trying to catch a feather in a windstorm.

Backpedaling faster than Dyphestive could run, Grey Cloak said, "If you could only see yourself. So flustered and red. If you had horns, you would make a fine bull."

Dyphestive stopped, wiped the sweat from his brow, and took a knee, gasping.

Grey Cloak strolled up to him and said, "What is the matter? Are you all out of wind? I have plenty."

"I'll get you," Dyphestive said as he fought to catch his breath. He clutched his chest and continued panting heavily.

Grey Cloak leaned toward him and said, "No, brother, you'll never get me. Face it—you are too slow. But don't feel bad. Everyone is, compared to me."

Dyphestive said, wheezing, "I'll... get... you."

Grey Cloak casually looked up at the mountain and said, "I think I can handle the trek all by myself."

Dyphestive punched his brother in the gut. Grey Cloak hopped a half step back but not before Dyphestive's big knuckles connected with muscles. He doubled over and half danced, half staggered backward.

Then Dyphestive charged Grey Cloak and tackled him to the ground. He had only pretended to be winded and was more than fine. "Now who has who?"

Grey Cloak kneed him in the jaw and squirmed out from underneath him then bounced up and tried to kick him in the ribs, but Dyphestive caught his foot and twisted him to the ground.

"Let go of me, oaf!" Grey Cloak kicked Dyphestive in the face with the bottom of his boot.

With a handful of his brother's cloak, Dyphestive hung on.

Grey Cloak twisted out of his cloak then used it to bind

Dyphestive's hands. "You won't be hitting anyone now." He groaned.

"What's the matter? Is your belly hurting?" Dyphestive kicked at his brother.

As Grey Cloak danced away, coins fell out of his pockets. He plucked them from the ground.

Dyphestive noticed that the purse Tanlin had given Grey Cloak was still sitting near the campfire. He lifted an eyebrow and made a chopping motion with his bound hands. The cloak tried with coinage. He tore it off his hands and fanned it like he was shaking out a blanket. Dozens of coins and gemstones fell out. "It looks like somebody fared better than they made out."

Grey Cloak smiled guiltily. "What can I say? I'm greedy. It's a thing. Can I have my cloak?"

Dyphestive threw the cloak at him. "Take it."

Grey Cloak caught the cloak, whipped it in the air in a showy fashion, and hung it on his shoulders. He started picking up his coins and gems. "It's been awhile since we had a tussle like that. I was beginning to wonder if you still had the same fight in you."

"I always have fight in me. I just don't show it like you do." He dusted off his pants. "I'll stick with you, but I don't want to go back in that temple. I think we would be fools if we did so."

"Perhaps you're right. Maybe we will make a go of it some other day. Do you want to catch up with the others?"

"Do you mean that?"

"I can see it means a lot to you. Though I think now we would do fine without them."

Dyphestive attached his iron sword to his saddle. "But they voted us out. What makes you think that they'll take us back?"

"They are old people. We are young. It'll appeal to their parental nature. They won't be able to resist taking us back." He picked up the purse Tanlin had given him and hid it under his cloak. "And by using a convincing degree of sincerity, we'll both be in their good graces again." He offered his hand to Dyphestive. "Besides, this is far better than being at Dark Mountain. Is all well?"

Dyphestive took Grey Cloak's hand and squeezed it with a crushing grip. "All is well. Promise me you'll behave yourself."

The elf winced, pulled his hand free, and said, "You know I can't do that."

"I know." He noticed Grey Cloak staring at his mouth. "What?"

"The tooth that Browning knocked out... I think it's growing back."

Dyphestive licked his upper row of teeth and smiled. "I know. Watch out, sweet corn. Here I come."

48

IT WAS NIGHTTIME, AND ZORA WAS SITTING AT A TABLE in an inn in Red Bone with Tanlin, Tatiana, and Browning. They were picking at the food on their table. Zora ate little.

"Get it out, Zora," Browning said. "Everyone here can see that your hair is about to catch fire."

"Well, it should be obvious." She pushed her plate away, picked up her goblet of wine, and drank. "How could all of you vote against Grey Cloak and Dyphestive? They saved our lives." She eyed Tanlin. "I'm most disappointed in you."

"You know that if we don't have discipline, we'll have disorder," Tatiana said. The elven mystic sat upright, like an all-knowing queen, and put her hand on Zora's forearm. "I can understand the reason for your attachment. But the situation will only worsen with Dalsay. He and the elf are oil and water. We must maintain continuity."

"That's Dalsay talking," Browning said.

"It is not. I'm a freethinker," Tatiana fired back.

"Hah. You sound just like him, and you know it. Of course, we know the reason for that, don't we?" Browning slugged down his tankard of ale and tipped his chair back on two legs.

"I don't know what you mean," Tatiana said.

"Now who's lying?" Browning asked.

Tatiana gave Browning an icy look and flicked a finger. Browning's chair fell back and crashed to the floor. The barmaids passing in his wake jumped.

"It's fine! It's fine!" Browning held up his tankard. "I didn't spill a drop. It emptied into my belly." He rolled up to a knee, set his chair up, and sat back down. Then he slammed his tankard on the table. "You owe me a drink."

"You didn't spill a drop," Tatiana said.

"It's the principle." Browning flagged down a barmaid.

A waiter came over. "Another tankard?"

"Uh, yes, but I want that cute woman with the bouncy locks to fetch it, if you don't mind, son," Browning said.

"I'll let her know." The server hustled away.

"Don't run off our server," Tatiana said. "I liked him."

"Me too," Zora agreed.

Browning threw up his hands. "As long as you're buying, you can be served by whoever you want." He pointed at Tatiana. "But you're only changing the subject."

"Yes, you and Dalsay aren't fooling anyone," Tanlin said as he cut off a small portion of ham. "How much time have you been spending together outside of Talon?"

Tatiana deflated. "Is it that obvious?"

"Not until now," Zora said.

Browning erupted in laughter. "Bwah-ha-ha! We tricked you into admitting it. It's confirmed now. I knew it."

Tatiana's cheeks turned rosy. "I hate all of you."

"It's not as if anyone is going to say anything to Dalsay about it," Zora said. She patted Tatiana's hand. "Your secret is safe with us." She tried to hold back a laugh. "Because I'd be too embarrassed to tell anyone, either."

"He's not that bad," Tatiana argued. "He's... he's handsome and kind. You don't know him like I do."

"Thank the dragons for that." Zora lifted her wine glass. "To Dalsay and Tatiana."

"Wait, I don't have a tankard yet," Browning said.

A buxom waitress arrived with her hands filled with two tankards of ale and handed them to him.

"Thank you, milady!" He lifted up both of his tankards. "To Tatiana and Dalsay! May the flames of your love burn for all eternity, or at least until Dalsay's frosty stare ices them over!"

Everyone at the table cackled with laughter. Even Tatiana couldn't fight back a chuckle.

Zora leaned over the table, clutching her belly. "My stomach hurts. And I thought those ghouls' claws were painful." She reached back and rubbed her shoulder.

An odd silence fell over the table.

"You never told us how you were healed," Tatiana said. "I would like to know more about it. Ghoul marks are not easily vanquished and are most often fatal, even for a mystic of my skill, and I have the amulet."

"I only remember the attack in the cavern. I thrust my daggers into a ghoul's belly. There were numbers, greater numbers, then nothing. All I felt was cold," Zora said. She shivered. "I don't remember going down the mountain. I don't remember seeing Grey Cloak or Dyphestive. I felt like I was trapped in a deep, dark, cold well."

"I know the feeling. My first marriage felt like that," Browning quipped. He elbowed Tatiana. "I bet you know the feeling too."

Tatiana rolled her eyes. "Please continue, Zora. Tell me about the hermit. Do you remember him? Do you remember the moment you were healed?"

"I felt a warm spring rise inside me. I gasped and spit out black bile." She made a sour face. "I remember a man, like a hermit. His hair was long, rusty, and stringy. His arms were scaly, like a serpent that's shedding. Diseased. In his brown eyes were flecks of gold. He didn't look like much, but then, for a moment, like in a dream, he was the most handsome man that I ever saw." She blinked. "I was whole after that. All of my faculties returned, but the hermit was gone."

A belt with empty dagger scabbards sailed over Browning's head and looped itself around the back of Zora's chair.

"Grey Cloak!" Zora said. He was standing beside Dyphestive, and she jumped out of her seat, ran to the other side of the table, and hugged the smirking elf and Dyphestive too. "What are you doing here?"

"Believe it or not, Dalsay sent me here to find all of you," he said.

"Now, I know you are lying," she said.

"He's not," Adanadel said. He'd come from the front of the tavern and put his hands on the shoulders of both striplings. "We ran into them on the way back to Wizard Watch and had a long talk. Dalsay suggests another vote. He and I vote to keep them in. But that's all up to the rest of you."

"You vouch for Dalsay?" Tanlin asked Adanadel.

"I do. You can clarify when we meet him at the Iron Hills pass," Adanadel said. "All in favor, say—"

"Aye," everyone sitting at the table said, along with Zora.

"I figured as much."

Adanadel pulled a chair to the table, and Grey Cloak and Dyphestive joined him.

"Dalsay is taking the dragon charm to Wizard Watch. While he does that, I'll fill you in on our way back to Raven Cliff. For now, let's eat and drink." He grabbed one of Browning's tankards. "To Talon!"

49

THREE DAYS LATER, THE COMPANY, LED BY ADANADEL, met Dalsay at the Iron Hills pass. They sold the horses, which Browning called goblin meat, and carried their gear in packs. Dyphestive hauled the bulk of the load, carrying two packs at once, including his two-handed sword. They entered the hills north of where they exited the first time.

Grey Cloak spent much of his time talking to Zora and Tanlin. The rogues said they couldn't believe that Dalsay had changed his mind.

"I'm glad you are with us, elf, and I'm not entirely surprised," Tanlin said. He had his hands around the straps of his pack as they traversed the hills. "Dalsay can be unpredictable at times."

"And I can be convincing at times," Grey Cloak said.

They were walking behind the rest of the group. The

same as before, Adanadel and Browning were leading the way, followed by Dalsay and Tatiana. "Besides, you'll need me in case you run into more goblins."

"Yes, you were such a big help the last time," Zora commented. Her dagger belt's scabbards had been refilled with new steel that she'd bought back in Red Bone. She patted the handles. "Hopefully you won't have to borrow them again."

With Browning and Zora's help, Grey Cloak had equipped himself with a longsword and a dagger that he'd reluctantly bought with his own chips. He fingered the handles. "These goblin slayers will have to do."

"Right," she said. "What else did you and Dalsay speak about?"

"Adanadel did most of the talking. I think that we were being tested."

"*You* were being tested," Dyphestive said as he hoofed it up a steep incline in the hills.

Grey Cloak shrugged. "It might be as he says." He jumped over a fallen log and landed beside Zora. "It's refreshing to know that you missed me."

"I was worried," she said.

"That wasn't a worried hug that you gave me back in the tavern. That was an I-missed-you embrace," he said.

"You ooze with overconfidence."

"It does fit me like a glove." He grinned at her. He was glad they'd come back, not only because of Zora but mostly.

"When we get back to Raven Cliff, how about you take me out to dinner."

Zora laughed. "I don't have the inclination."

"After all that we have been through. I saved your life."

"No, the hermit did."

"He's a dear friend of mine."

"Phew!" Zora fanned her pretty face. "The manure is getting deep over here."

Tanlin cleared his throat. "Let's focus on getting out of these hills, shall we? Especially you, Grey Cloak. You take matters too lightly. Didn't you and Dalsay come to some sort of understanding about your frivolous attitude?"

"Yes," Dyphestive said.

"Frivolous attitude, yes, indeed," Grey Cloak said. "But it was only *frivolous* conversation that I was engaging in." He moved away from Zora. "But I digress. I'll keep my ears bent for the sound of goblins."

The company crested one of the higher elevations in the hills just past midday, and Adanadel stopped them for a rest.

"We are only a day away from the plains. We haven't spotted any signs of goblins, either. There is a gap in the hills a few leagues below us. We should be safe once we reach that spot."

"We have no reason to believe that they are searching for us," Browning said. "Just because we killed a goblin chieftain doesn't mean that we started a war. Even so, they might have moved on or cast the blame elsewhere. They are impulsive little mud balls."

Dalsay rubbed the palms of his hands with his thumbs. His eyes were fixed on the sky, and his gaze was spacey. "These hills are alive with them. I can feel it. War drums beat beneath my feet." His head moved slowly from side to side. "Stay alert for any sign."

A guttural hungry baying carried through the treetops, and everyone looked up.

Dyphestive stood. "Is that a sign?"

"No, that's a goblin war hound." Adanadel rushed down the path they'd come from and looked down the hill. "They must have caught our scent. I can hear them."

Dalsay joined the former monarch's knight at the crest of the hill, and Grey Cloak ran to the mage's side and followed his gaze. The sound of footsteps racing through the hills came from far below, hundreds of footsteps and rattling bones. His heart raced. Several goblin war hounds, huge dogs covered in mange, darted into view.

Dalsay turned and faced the company. "Run!" Balls of fire erupted from his fingertips and shot into the trees. Maples, pines, and oaks caught fire. Flames jumped from branch to branch, and the forest blazed.

"Follow me," Adanadel said. He angled down the hill at full speed.

The company zigzagged through the forest, Browning huffing and puffing. Tatiana chanted as she ran, holding her magic amulet up. It burned brightly like the sun, and the leaves they ran over turned to smoke and left a growing cloud trail behind them. The howling of the war hounds became louder.

Grey Cloak had no trouble keeping pace with the others. He glanced back over his shoulder. It was smoke and trees as far as he could see. But already, some of the members of the party were panting. They ran on, pushing themselves to the limits, seeking safety in the plains of civilization.

Two war dogs dashed out of the smoke. The bloodthirsty beasts slavered from their oversized jaws and raced alongside them.

"Keep running!" Dalsay commanded. Fiery balls of green energy shot from his hands, striking the hounds midstride.

The dogs' bodies erupted into four-legged flames. They ran on, wobbling on burning limbs, and died.

The company had made it half a league when they came to an overlook and stopped. Scores of goblins were gathered at the bottom the hill, blocking the passage north and east.

Adanadel caught his breath and said, "They've boxed us in. They knew exactly where to chase us."

"The goblins aren't without their tricks," Dalsay said. "Go west. It's the only choice we have."

"Why don't we fight them?" Dyphestive asked.

"Over one hundred goblins and their hounds," Browning said as he gasped. "Even if we killed half of them, they would shred us. We need good ground, Adanadel, if we are going to fight!"

"I know!" Adanadel took the lead again, moving fast in his heavy armor, as if it were clothing. He led them into a natural channel made from rocks and trees. It sloped upward to the wide mouth of a shallow cave. "This is it."

Tatiana's amulet had left a trail of smoke behind them that carried through the trees.

Browning was clasping his side and sweating buckets. "Fine by me. I'm ready to die right here. I would rather fight than run."

"No one's dying," Zora said.

"Tell that to the goblins," Browning fired back.

Dyphestive dropped his packs and stood in front of the cave, brandishing the iron sword. Adanadel and Browning flanked him.

Adanadel drew a longsword and a dagger and kissed the steel of his blade. "May the might of the monarchs aid us."

"Let's kill some goblins." Browning pulled out his broadsword and held up his buckler. "Before they kill us first."

The sinister cackling and ravenous cries of the goblins increased. The smoke began to thin. War hounds were the first to advance. Their heads hung low, and drool dripped over their canine teeth to the ground.

Slowly, the goblins appeared a few dozen yards away, a few at first, carrying spears, axes, and small swords. Then the number grew from a dozen to scores. Like shrubbery, their dirty bodies filled the forest, hemming the company in. Two large chieftains were among them, their fiendish yellow eyes fastened on Dyphestive's sword.

Grey Cloak was standing by his brother's side and said, "I'm beginning to think that rejoining Talon wasn't such a good idea. What about you?"

The ten-foot-tall goblin chieftains stepped forward. One was missing an eye, and the other was as bald as an eagle.

The one missing an eye was carrying a war hammer as tall as a man, and he said, "You killed my brothers. My brood. I will feast on your flesh tonight." He spread his arms wide. "We will all dine on your bones tonight!"

The goblins gave ear-splitting war cries, beat their weapons together, and rattled the bones of the dead they adorned themselves with.

"What are we going to do, Dalsay?" Tatiana asked.

"There is only one thing that we can do against a horde like that." The intense mage removed something wrapped in sackcloth from his pack. It was a figurine made of black jade, shaped like a nondescript person and covered in arcane carvings.

"No!" Tatiana said. "You swore that you'd never bring

that cursed thing with you again. Have you forgotten what happened the last time?"

"I didn't have a choice the last time either," Dalsay said as he set the figurine on the ground.

"Whatever it is, use it," Grey Cloak said. "How bad can it be?"

"I'll tell you how bad. The last time he used it, the person he summoned killed most of our party," Browning said.

"But the Figurine of Heroes has aided us many times too," Adanadel added.

"You mean Figurine of Horrors," Tatiana fired back. She grabbed Dalsay's arm. "I beg of you, don't use it."

"I won't watch the goblins take you away. Or any of us die at their hands. I'm sorry, Tatiana. I must risk it," Dalsay said.

"What does it do?" Grey Cloak asked.

"It summons a person or creature from another realm," Adanadel said.

"What realm?" he asked.

"Any realm," Tatiana answered.

Dalsay muttered mystic words, and the inches-high figurine started to spew black-and-gray smoke.

Tatiana's jaw clenched. "Be ready. Be ready to die."

50 HARBOR LAKE

EPILOGUE

AT MIDDAY, Rhonna ambled into the city called Harbor Lake, a thriving lakeside community. She walked down the boardwalk, where watercrafts of all sizes were sailing on the massive lake. Huge fishing boats were hauling in crabs, lobsters, and clams. The smell of fish grilling over fire pits made her stomach growl.

At the end of one of the numerous boardwalks that lined the lake was a set of steps that led down to the beach. She picked up the pace over the sand and rocks, not stopping until she came upon rows of waterside cottages made of stone, then she marched up to one that had a red wooden door.

A cute little half-orc girl opened the door and peeked through the crack. Her eyes grew wide, and she jumped back. "Mommy! Mommy! It's a dwarf. A lady dwarf! He-he!"

A pleasant-looking woman opened the door. She wiped her hands on her apron and said, "Rhonna! How good it is to see you!"

"Sarah," Rhonna said. "It's good to see you too."

The little girl was peeking from behind Sarah's dress and giggling uncontrollably.

"I'm sorry. Little Lylith hasn't seen many dwarves, especially a woman." Sarah picked her daughter up. "So what is going on?"

"I need to talk to Lythlenion."

Sarah eyed her. "It sounds serious. Is it?"

"I didn't come all this way for your cooking." Rhonna's nose crinkled. "I remember the last time."

"Mommy's cooking is terrible," Lylith said.

"That's because your father married me for my looks, not my cooking." Sarah kissed her daughter and set her down. "Run down to the beach and check the crab crates."

"Yes, Mommy." Lylith grinned at Rhonna. "Bye, Dwarfie."

"Lythlenion is behind the house, gardening. All he does is talk about his lilies." Sarah sighed and said, "I probably shouldn't say this, but he could use a trip, if you know what I mean."

Rhonna raised the corner of her mouth in a half smile. "I'll look after him."

"Should I ask or not?"

"I'm looking for a couple of boys that are missing from my farm. I thought Lythlenion might want to help out."

Sarah nodded. "I see. Let me go and tell him that you are—"

"Rhonna! Ha! I heard everything!" A forty-something orc with a medium build and long blond hair rushed from somewhere in the cottage to the entrance. He had a modestly trimmed white beard and was strapping on a breastplate. Throwing a large rucksack over Rhonna's head, he said to Sarah, "Help me with this armor, love."

Sarah buckled the leather straps on the side.

Lythlenion kissed her. "Thank you, dear. I'll see Lylith on my way out. Miss you already," he said without looking back as he joined Rhonna.

"Oh, Lythlenion," Sarah called. She was cradling a heavy-looking war mace in her slender arms. "I believe you forgot something."

Lythlenion ran back and grabbed it and kissed her again. "Thank you, dearest. I'm sure I'll be back soon. Very soon!"

Sarah smiled and waved. "You'd better be."

They went down to the beach, where Lythlenion sang Lylith a sweet goodbye song, then they headed toward the docks.

"Oh, I'm so glad you came. I love Sarah with all of my heart, but—"

"She can't cook. I know."

They ambled down the boardwalk planks.

"I think she does it on purpose." He rubbed his beard, which was a mix of white and straw colored. "How can you cook every day and not get better?"

"*You* could cook."

"I *do* cook. See what I mean? She's gaming me." He put his hand on Rhonna's shoulder. "So what is going on? Troll trouble? Halfling wizards? Maybe a treasure quest?"

"I've been raising a couple of boys—well, striplings now. They disappeared."

Lythlenion scratched his soft-featured but rugged face. "If you were raising them, well, it's not that surprising, given the taskmaster that you are. I would probably run away too."

"It's no wonder that Sarah didn't mind you leaving."

He shrugged.

"A few days ago, someone came looking for them. Someone we know. Someone you know."

"Who?"

"Drysis."

He stopped in the middle of the boardwalk and said, "Oh." He swallowed. "So she wanted the boys?"

"She's a Doom Rider now. She rides gourns." Rhonna could see Lythlenion's blue eyes dancing. "She means business."

"Of course, if she's in league with the forces of Dark Mountain. Where are the boys?"

"I don't know. That's why I came to find you. You and Slender. My gut tells me something big is brewing with these striplings. They're different."

"You think they are naturals, don't you?"

"I didn't, but I do now." She continued walking. "Why else would Doom Riders want them?"

"Maybe they stole something."

"No, that's not it. They want the striplings. And they'll do anything to find them."

"I see." Lythlenion swung his war mace onto his shoulder. "So where's Griff?"

"Drysis killed him."

WILL the heroes survive the battles against the goblins in the Iron Hills?

Who are the Doom Riders? What do they really want?

PLEASE DON'T FORGET **to leave a review on book 1, Blood Brothers. They are a huge help! Thanks! LINK!!**

DOWNLOAD BOOK #2, Black Frost, and find out now!

Black Frost: Dragon Wars - Book 2 Link

Amazon US

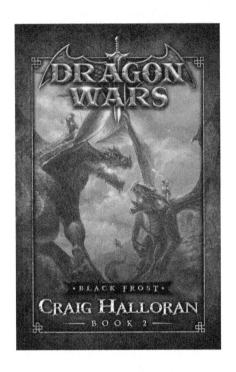

Be sure to sign up for my newsletter and get 3 FREE books, includes inside story on Grey Cloak and Dyphestive's past at:

WWW.DRAGONWARSBOOKS.COM.

TEACHERS AND STUDENTS, if you would like to order paperback copies for you library or classroom, email craig@thedarkslayer.com to receive a special discount.

GEAR UP in this Dragon Wars body armor enchanted with a +2 Coolness factor/+4 at Gaming Conventions. Sizes range from halfling (Small) to Ogre (XXL). LINK See image below. www.society6.com

SCROLL DOWN TO learn more about Craig Halloran and his other books. And don't forget to sign up for his newsletter and download 3 FREE books, including the Dragon Wars Prequel. WWW. DRAGONWARSBOOKS.COM

ABOUT THE AUTHOR

Thanks for reading Blood Brothers: Dragon Wars - Book 1. If you would, please leave a review. They are a huge help to me! Here is a link to book 1.

CRAIG@THEDARKSLAYER.COM

Also, please drop me a line anytime or check in with me on FB at The Darkslayer Report. I always reply to all of my readers and enjoy the conversation.

*Check me out on BookBub and follow: HalloranOn-BookBub.

*I'd love it if you would subscribe to my mailing list: www.craighalloran.com and get FREE books!

*On Facebook, you can find me at The Darkslayer Report or Craig Halloran.

*Twitter, Twitter, Twitter. I am there too: www.twitter.com/CraigHalloran.

*And of course, you can always email me at craig@thedarkslayer.com.

See my book lists below!

ALSO BY CRAIG HALLORAN

Craig Halloran resides with his family outside his hometown of Charleston, West Virginia. When he isn't entertaining mankind, he is seeking adventure, working out, or watching sports. To learn more about him, go to www.thedarkslayer.com.

Check out all my great stories...

Free Books

The Darkslayer: Brutal Beginnings

Nath Dragon—Quest for the Thunderstone

Dragon Wars

Blood Brothers

Black Frost

Sky Rider

Iron Bones

Dark Mountain

Monarch City

Terror Maze

Grey Cloak

The Chronicles of Dragon Series 1 (10-book series)

The Hero, the Sword and the Dragons (Book 1)

Dragon Bones and Tombstones (Book 2)

Terror at the Temple (Book 3)

Clutch of the Cleric (Book 4)

Hunt for the Hero (Book 5)

Siege at the Settlements (Book 6)

Strife in the Sky (Book 7)

Fight and the Fury (Book 8)

War in the Winds (Book 9)

Finale (Book 10)

Boxset 1–5

Boxset 6–10

Collector's Edition 1–10

Tail of the Dragon, The Chronicles of Dragon, Series 2 (10-book series)

Tail of the Dragon #1

Claws of the Dragon #2

Battle of the Dragon #3

Eyes of the Dragon #4

Flight of the Dragon #5

Trial of the Dragon #6

Judgement of the Dragon #7

Wrath of the Dragon #8

Power of the Dragon #9

Hour of the Dragon #10

Boxset 1–5

Boxset 6–10

Collector's Edition 1–10

The Odyssey of Nath Dragon Series (New Series) (Prequel to Chronicles of Dragon)

Exiled

Enslaved

Deadly

Hunted

Strife

The Darkslayer Series 1 (6-book series)

Wrath of the Royals (Book 1)

Blades in the Night (Book 2)

Underling Revenge (Book 3)

Danger and the Druid (Book 4)

Outrage in the Outlands (Book 5)

Chaos at the Castle (Book 6)

Boxset 1–3

Boxset 4–6

Omnibus 1–6

The Darkslayer: Bish and Bone, Series 2 (10-book series)

Bish and Bone (Book 1)

Black Blood (Book 2)

Red Death (Book 3)

Lethal Liaisons (Book 4)

Torment and Terror (Book 5)

Brigands and Badlands (Book 6)

War in the Wasteland (Book 7)

Slaughter in the Streets (Book 8)

Hunt of the Beast (Book 9)

The Battle for Bone (Book 10)

Boxset 1–5

Boxset 6–10

Bish and Bone Omnibus (Books 1–10)

CLASH OF HEROES: Nath Dragon meets The Darkslayer mini series

Book 1

Book 2

Book 3

The Henchmen Chronicles

The King's Henchmen

The King's Assassin

The King's Prisoner

The King's Conjurer

The King's Enemies

The Gamma Earth Cycle

Escape from the Dominion

Flight from the Dominion

Prison of the Dominion

The Supernatural Bounty Hunter Files (10-book series)

Smoke Rising: Book 1

I Smell Smoke: Book 2

Where There's Smoke: Book 3

Smoke on the Water: Book 4

Smoke and Mirrors: Book 5

Up in Smoke: Book 6

Smoke Signals: Book 7

Holy Smoke: Book 8

Smoke Happens: Book 9

Smoke Out: Book 10

Boxset 1–5

Boxset 6–10

Collector's Edition 1–10

Zombie Impact Series

Zombie Day Care: Book 1

Zombie Rehab: Book 2

Zombie Warfare: Book 3

Boxset: Books 1–3

OTHER WORKS & NOVELLAS

The Red Citadel and the Sorcerer's Power

Made in the USA
Monee, IL
29 March 2021